DAY
NINETEEN

PAUL ALONGI SR.

authorHOUSE®

AuthorHouse™
1663 Liberty Drive
Bloomington, IN 47403
www.authorhouse.com
Phone: 1 (800) 839-8640

Published by AuthorHouse 08/30/2016

ISBN: 978-1-5246-2744-7 (sc)
ISBN: 978-1-5246-2745-4 (hc)
ISBN: 978-1-5246-2743-0 (e)

Library of Congress Control Number: 2016914369

Print information available on the last page.

This enjoyable book is dedicated to my six grandchildren, Kara, Ryan, Michael, Matthew, Jack, and Eric. All except Eric were born on the nineteenth of different months. Eric, the youngest, was born on the twentieth, eight hours removed from the nineteenth. My deceased wife, Toni, of fifty-seven years; my son, Paul, and daughter-in-law, Kim; my daughter, Gina, and son-in-law, Tom, have been my life, and for them I thank my God and Maker.

NOTE

Life was never easy for the Braden boys. Right from the outset they had to endure one episode after another. Unfortunately, tragedy usually occurred and forever was unexplainable. Their friendships and relationships were continually being challenged and at times tarnished by others who were envious of their success.

The story of the younger brother, Chad, illustrates a life replete with obstacles and reversals. However, you will be able to see that he was strong enough to overcome those ever occurring crises. Chad was different from Pat, his older brother. His many loves were exciting but always burdensome. On the other hand, Pat dedicated his life and soul to God.

They both shared a strong family thread and brotherly love, and those appeared to be the factors in reconciling their totally opposite careers. Oddly, they were both born on February nineteen but four years apart.

Chad became a naval intelligence officer, cloaked in secrecy and conspiracies, always targeted on the potential of our enemies to cause havoc to the lifestyle and freedoms of our society. He was up to the challenges but suffered the failures that accompanies such a position.

You will also discover that Chad's life was filled with the same human frailties possessed by others. He always attempted to persevere, but he would not overcome many enormous risks. All of this became apparent as Chad awaited being executed in nineteen days for the murder of his fiancée and her father. You are urged to discover whether the collective faith of the brothers was enough to ward off the gas chamber and return him to a life of service to our beloved country or suffer death as a consequence.

CHAPTER 1

Rear Admiral Chad Braden (Ret), a decorated naval hero, age sixty-four, lay in a bed at Johns Hopkins in a semi-coma, suffering from multiple stab wounds. His son Mark, age thirty-two, had originally admitted his dad for treatment of the dementia that was slowly creeping throughout his once extra-sharp mind.

Two days later a dark complected man of Middle Eastern descent, disguised as an orderly, stole into the admiral's private room and slashed and stabbed him with a large knife. Fortunately, Braden was awake and alert enough to fend off the attack to his throat, but he could not avert the stabs to his chest and stomach. The bleeding was extensive and caused him to lose consciousness.

Help came when Nurse Candice, who was watching the monitor and witnessed the attack as soon as it began, immediately called security, who dispatched four guards. They didn't have far to go as their command center was on the same floor.

As they rushed into the room, the guards were confronted by this evil person wildly swinging his weapon. The four of them rushed the assailant and overcame him. While on the floor, he yelled, "Death to the Braden pig!"

As Chad languished in a semi-coma, his mind was full of memories from his boyhood days in Quenton, Maryland. There were four in his family, including his brother, Pat; his loving and caring father; and his mother, who never wanted to be a mom. She was cold, unemotional, and distant. Despite her, it was a happy home because of his father's devotion to the boys.

Chad's mom and dad, Mitzi and Chad Sr., were childhood sweethearts and attended grammar school and high school together. They were married immediately after graduation against their parents' wishes. However, Grandpa Clark, Mitzi's dad, a successful attorney and judge, worth millions, volunteered to finance their educations at the University of Maryland. Pat came along while they were in their second year, and Grandpa Clark supported the family, making it possible for Chad Sr. to later have a successful law practice with Jamie Robbins as his partner. Mitzi Braden became a psychologist specializing in child behavior, a major contradiction if ever there was one.

Quenton had a population of about twenty thousand that was dwindling by the minute as the younger people were making their way to the larger cities. The homes were all colonial style built on very large lots with an abundance of trees and grass. The streets were mainly narrow and illuminated at night by antique lantern lights. The center of town was pristine and old. It was six blocks long with two banks, a bar and grill, movie theater with one wide screen, a drug store with a fifties décor—including a sweetshop and fountain—hair salon, and two boarding houses. South of the center was the pride and joy of Quenton, a new high school and a three thousand-seat sparkling new stadium. It was this setting that framed Chad's boyhood life.

He was the celebrated quarterback at the high school and earned all-state honors. Many colleges were trying to recruit him, but his dad encouraged him as a scholar athlete to select Ocean Naval Academy. While at Quenton High, Chad not only excelled in football but had a superior intellect that proved to be his best quality. He had the looks and celebrity status that attracted girls without any effort.

His social life ceased when Sherry came into the picture. She was beautiful and spunky and had a body punctuated by a rather large bust. This pretty redhead was captain of the cheerleading squad. She had been the girlfriend of Jimmy Spanks, the starting quarterback, during Chad's freshman and sophomore years. Jimmy became history when he was caught by the vice principal with a gun in his locker. It was rumored that someone had ratted on him.

Following the suspensions and within a very short time, the Spanks family reluctantly decided to move out to Colorado.

One cold and wintry night in late November, the team was returning from a playoff game with Gabriel High. The mood on the bus was sullen because of a close loss that resulted from Chad throwing a late interception that was returned for the winning TD. He was seated by himself staring out into the dark night when Sherry slid into the next seat.

He was totally surprised as she placed her hand on his upper thigh and whispered in his ear, "I'll be waiting for you outside the gym door. Take a good shower because I want to go to the bluff with you."

She placed her hand on his groin and said, "More to come."

He became fully aroused and was consumed with anxiety.

The bluff was five miles from the Crowder Quarry. It was a deserted area that was known as the favorite make-out spot for the high school kids. There were so many different areas to park, so it was possible to be alone and apart from other cars. Added to the isolation of the bluff was the absence of any lights, which made the night much darker.

Sherry was right outside the door as promised. She was wearing her short cheerleader skirt with a loose-fitting sweater.

Chad said, "Let's go," and off they went in his 1980 blue Plymouth.

Upon arrival at the bluff, they began kissing and petting. When Chad realized she wasn't wearing a bra, he immediately immersed himself in her breasts. This made Sherry so excited that she uttered, "I want to go all the way with you, and I'll show how I want it."

She then gathered him and guided him as a teacher with years of instruction, step by step, until that moment of ultimate satisfaction. For the first time in his life he felt like a man.

He left her off a block away from her home as she requested and proceeded down to his house on Founder Terrace. As he was turning onto his street, lights were flashing by his house.

Pat was sitting on the curb. When he saw Chad, he ran to his car. Pat said, "You don't want to go in there. Mom and Dad are gone."

Chad felt faint and nauseated and couldn't believe what Pat was saying. He got out of the car and both brothers embraced, overcome with grief.

After several minutes, Pat said, "I came home about nine and realized something was wrong. The house was totally dark. There was an eerie silence. I opened the door and saw Mom lying in a pool of blood.

"She wasn't moving, and I knew she was dead. She was in the foyer, which led me to believe she was trying to run out of the house. About ten feet away Dad was on the floor with a gunshot to the head. There was no doubt he was the shooter. Then I saw the note pinned to his shirt. It said, 'Guys, I can't live like this anymore; please forgive me.'"

Chad turned his brother and said, "What do you think he meant?"

Pat shook his head and sat down on the curb to steady himself. With his voice cracking, he said, "We'll have to ask Jamie and Ginny Robbins. They should know."

*

What they didn't realize was that Ginny Robbins, the wife of their dad's law partner, had grown suspicious about her husband, Jamie's, fidelity. She hired Don Arons, a private detective who was well noted in that field. That was confirmed by the nature of the fees he charged.

Don, upon meeting Ginny, was taken with her movie star looks and couldn't believe that her husband was seeing another woman. She filled him in on Jamie's habits and asked that Don call her as soon as he had some results.

Don followed him for ten days without any event, except that he continually observed Jamie flirting with waitresses. However, he got lucky on the eleventh day. Jamie had gone to a Nike store at the outlet shops and was spotted speaking with a tall, lanky, beautiful blonde. The two embraced and walked out of the store together. Her red Mercury Marquis was parked next to Jamie's car. She slid into the passenger's seat and Jamie drove off to the Windsor Motel some twenty miles away.

Don followed them, and once at the motel, he called Ginny. When he described the blonde and her car, Don heard Ginny gasp.

Don asked, "Do you know her?"

Ginny answered yes.

Ginny then drove to the motel and met Don. She was very upset, crying and yelling, "How could they do this?"

Don gave the office clerk twenty dollars in exchange for a passkey, and together they walked to the first floor room that the couple had entered.

Ginny abruptly unlocked the door.

Jamie was in his shorts, and her best friend, Mitzi Braden, was in her pink bra and pants. Both were shocked to see her.

Ginny said in disbelief, "How could you do this to us?" and slammed the door. She turned to Don and cried, "I'll see you later!"

She ran to her car and took off in a fury.

CHAPTER 2

CHAPTER 2

The next day Ginny met Chad Sr. at the Lawrence Coffee Shop on Main Street, a block and a half from the law office. Ginny noted that he was pale and morose. He wasn't his old bubbly self and appeared to sense the bad news that was coming.

He was out of character when he abruptly whispered, "What's up?"

Finally she uttered, "Chad, I'm sorry, but these are pictures that my investigator took yesterday at the Windsor Motel."

He picked them up, looked at them, and flung them on the table. Then he stood up and walked out without saying a word.

Ginny didn't like the look on his face and was concerned that she had confronted him.

She decided to contact Mitzi and tell her about the meeting and her husband's reaction. This was to no avail as Mitzi wasn't home or answering her phone.

Ginny's next decision was to go to the law office and seek Jamie out. He wasn't there, and Jeanie, their girl Friday, didn't know where both her bosses had gone. Ginny went home and wished for the best.

*

The joint funeral at St. John's was held on a bleak wintry day with occasional snow flurries.

Most of the Maryland politicians showed up, no doubt paying their respect to Chad Sr., who had been Quenton's mayor for three terms.

Both boys were seated in the front row next to their parents' caskets. Grandpa Clark was right behind them with Jamie Robbins and his very attractive daughter, Jeri. During the funeral, Chad kept daydreaming about Jeri. On a scale of one to ten, Jeri was a perfect ten in looks and sexy body. He felt guilty thinking about Jeri with the caskets right next to him but could not bring himself to stop.

Each year the two families would share a six-bedroom colonial summer home in Ocean City, Maryland. It was located right on the water and made it possible for the wives and children to enjoy the whole summer. The men would commute three days a week to the office and spend long weekends at the shore. As a result, Ginny and Mitzi became very close.

They both were very pretty and enjoyed high-fashion clothing. Most of their time was spent shopping for themselves and their kids. They had a lot in common, especially since both were avid shoppers. While the kids were young, they gave full rein to the nanny/housekeeper/ cook who lived with them at the summer home.

Jeri and Chad were about the same age and were supervised until they became teenagers.

They were like brother and sister, always hanging out together. Pat was a loner and kept to himself. The boys loved Ginny Robbins as she continually doted on them, something their mom did not do.

Conversely, they couldn't stand Jamie Robbins. He drank a lot, was loud, and flirted with every female he came into contact with.

Chad Sr. was the opposite. He managed to spend his free time with the kids and went out of his way to favor Jeri. The four of them loved to fish, especially Jeri, who seemed to have a natural affinity for the water. On one of the trips Pat accidentally fell into the ocean, and Jeri calmly jumped in with a float and gave it to Pat. They both were able to safely get back to the boat.

Things changed when Jeri and Chad Jr. reached puberty. Their relationship became sexually intense. Both realized there was a mutual physical attraction, and Chad had made it rather obvious that he was obsessed with her evolving body.

The whole situation came to a grinding halt when they were fourteen. Jeri asked Chad to come to her bedroom and whispered, "No one is in the house. Both our moms are out for the day, and there is something I want to show you."

He immediately followed her up the winding stairs to her room on the third level. When they got inside, Jeri took off her top, exposing those pink and hard nipples. "I know you've been looking at my body, especially my tits. Now you can hold them in your hands."

With that he jumped to the offer and caressed her breasts with his hands and lips.

They then kissed and steadily pet each other for the next few days. These encounters came to a complete end when Jamie Robbins walked in on them. He was supposed to be working but came down to the shore earlier than usual.

They were totally humiliated when Jamie slapped both of them in the face and said firmly, "That's it. Tomorrow we go home, and never again will we share our vacations together."

From that point on, the two families never socialized again.

When Chad looked up next, Jamie was into his eulogy of his former partner. "He was a loving and caring partner," he said, going into details about his life and career.

Noticeably absent from the funeral was Ginny Robbins. Jamie had said to the boys that she had caught a virus.

After the services were over, Jeri said to Pat and Chad, "Why don't you come back to my house?"

They did and were confused by Jamie's behavior. He isolated himself in one room and barely came out to advise the boys. They wanted to know what was in store for them, and he wasn't helping.

Ginny, who seemed to have made a remarkable recovery, was sitting in the dining room listening to their concerns.

Both boys turned to her, and she responded weakly, "Jamie has to tell you, not me."

Jamie came out into the room about fifteen minutes later and said to them, "Let's leave everything for another day," and walked out of the house.

Both turned to Jeri and said, "What was that all about?"

She had a dumb look on her face and just shrugged, uttering, "I don't know."

CHAPTER 3

CHAPTER 3

Months later Chad was a midshipman at Ocean Naval Academy. The school stood on a large hill overlooking the vast Chesapeake Bay surrounded by the natural beauties of the planet. He was a totally different person now, affected by the death of his parents and had become more serious. Burdened with grief, he chose to follow through on his father's wish that he attend Ocean. His intent was to make a new life for himself.

Meanwhile, his brother, Pat, had entered the Christian Seminary in Baltimore and was looking forward to being ordained.

On the very first day of school he met Carl Tracka, his new roommate. Carl was the son of Polish immigrants from Chicago and was dark in complexion with thick black eyebrows. He had a nose that appeared to be chiseled onto his face. His uncle, Congressman George Koski, was responsible for getting Carl into Ocean. The fact that Carl was an all-state receiver helped also. Carl had been recruited by Notre Dame but chose the navy life. It was obvious why they had been put together, and it was hoped that their relationship would somehow spill onto the field.

Together they began to live those rigorous days of class, study, and practice. Chad always had had a special feeling when setting foot on the stadium grass. He was drawn to the spectacular beauty of the sun cradling against the skyline and the big trees in the nearby background. The coach often observed Chad doing that and labeled him a daydreamer.

Their everyday schedule was a real grind: class to study hall and then football. They were getting bombarded by the upperclassmen on the team who continually would try to haze them. Carl couldn't take it, because he thought it was so immature and would publicly explode.

Contrarily, Chad took it all in stride and would try to calm Carl. Sometime it worked, but not without a real effort by Chad. As time passed he came to understand his roommate was really secretive, silent, and mysterious. Whenever he spoke, it would be about himself or his uncle George. Chad would do his best to try to engage him in conversation about religion or politics to no avail. Carl would actually turn and walk away.

Once training camp was over, Chad was selected as the varsity backup quarterback, and Carl made the first team as the wide receiver. The season started with a loss to Colgate and progressively got worse. It escalated to seven more losses. Chad was depressed and disgusted about riding the bench. Most of his quarterbacking came during practice, which was frustrating. He was further anguished because Carl was having a great year despite the team losing all their games, because Carl was the team's leading receiver and playing every game.

This all changed when Chad got his big break in the last game against their archrival, Reynolds University. Johnny Mars, the starting quarterback, suffered a concussion late in the third quarter.

Coach Glenn turned to him and said, "Chad, this is your chance— make the most of it."

The score was thirteen to seven in favor of Reynolds. Ocean had not beaten Reynolds in the last six years.

He approached the huddle and said. "Jackson five."

They all looked at him as if he was crazy.

He said, "You heard me; let's go."

Chad then took the snap from Kit, his bulky center, sidestepped a blitzing linebacker, and threw a thirty yard touchdown pass to Carl. Before the game was over, Chad had thrown for 126 yards and two more touchdowns. The final score was twenty-eight to thirteen, and Ocean had reversed the losing streak.

The locker room was extra-jubilant after the game, and Chad was the center of attention.

Carl came up to Chad and didn't offer any congratulations. Instead, he said, "Let's go celebrate with the girls. I'll call them and have them meet us at our dorm. Is that okay with you?"

He nodded, and Carl took off.

They had been sneaking out after curfew and returning without being missed. Both would camp out at Chad's cousin Billy's house and operate from there. Usually Sherry would bring a blind date for Carl. However, this one time she brought Chad's old flame, Jeri Robbins. He was stunned, for the last thing he ever wanted was for Carl to fall in love with her. Chad hadn't seen her for a long time and couldn't take his eyes off her.

Jeri's body had matured, and her breasts were large and firm, a size most women would kill for. He kept remembering all the times he had held and caressed them before their vacation adventures were abruptly terminated.

Now Carl had a chance with her, to Chad's disadvantage. It pained him terribly.

After some self-examination, he figured out why Sherry had brought Jeri along on that first date. It went back to the senior prom, when he had dumped Sherry for Jeri. He had invited Sherry but blew her off when Jeri called and asked him to go with her. His excuse to Sherry was that they were like brother and sister and she needed a date. Sherry didn't take that too well and threw a temper tantrum, unexpectedly jolting Chad.

When Sherry first brought Jeri to meet Carl, he said to her, "I didn't know she was your friend."

"After graduation, we both volunteered at the hospital and became very friendly. She's pretty regular—except for her creepy father. Every time I go to her house and he's there, he continually stares at my body."

It became obvious that both girls were pissed at Chad for the events of prom night and wanted to punish him much more.

Chad then relived prom night in his mind. He entered Jeri's house and saw her walk down the winding stairway. She looked so sexy in a beautiful, low-cut pale green gown showing her cleavage.

When they got into the car, she immediately snuggled close to him and said, "Drive on, Chad."

He pulled out a flask of vodka mixed with tonic and they both drank until they were giddy. When they entered the gym it was decorated in black and white nightclub style. The prom was in full swing, and the room was vibrating with high energy.

Couples danced wildly. Chad took Jeri's hand and led her to the far side of the gym where his friends from the team were hanging out. He spotted Sherry dancing closely with his best friend, Davey Albert. Chad was staring at them when Jeri let go of his hand and went over to Artie Clark. She took his hand and dragged him onto the dance floor.

Meanwhile, Chad was standing alone, wondering what had just happened. All he could do was to wait for the next dance and pull her into his arms. He asked, "Why did you do that?"

She answered, "Because I caught you looking at Sherry."

Chad then said, "Let it go. Tonight is our night."

She then responded by putting her head on his shoulder, and for the rest of the night, they were like two love birds. Chad could see Sherry fuming, but frankly, he was not worried as he was enjoying Jeri's company.

At the end of the night Chad asked Jeri if they could park at the bluff.

Jeri said rather strongly, "Yes."

When they arrived, Chad reached over and kissed her with passion. She responded by releasing the strap to her gown, exposing her big breasts. Jeri took Chad's head and pushed his face down onto her nipples. He reacted by backing off, surprised by the aggressive move on her part.

She fastened her strap and said, "Please take me home."

He tried to explain, but she would not hear it.

On the way to her house, he heard her crying. That night ended whatever romantic feelings Jeri had for Chad, and she never talked to him again until she surfaced as Carl's date. Even then, the small talk between them just didn't make any sense.

CHAPTER 4

The girls showed up at the dorm about half past seven, and they all jumped in Chad's Plymouth. They drove to a bar that served food in the Little Italy section of Baltimore. After a couple of hours there, the group went to the harbor to the famous club, Max's by the Sea.

Three or four stingers later, they checked into the Marriott Inner Harbor. Chad was devastated when he witnessed Carl and Jeri going off to their room. He was upset that it was so easy for Carl to become intimate with the real girl of his dreams. Jeri was a full-grown beauty that any man would wish for, and here was Carl winning that prize without any effort at all.

As he and Sherry were approaching their room, Sherry turned to him and said, "What's wrong?"

He then grabbed her and kissed her and said, "Nothing you can't cure."

After a couple of hours of pure sex, the two couples met two hours later in the lobby and decided to call it a night. By now it was a quarter to two in the morning.

As they were heading back to the dorm on Highway 95, an eighteen wheeler traveling north crossed the divider and struck the car by Chad's side. The impact caused the car to bounce off and strike a Cadillac. Chad was pinned to the wheel while the others were only shaken.

As they were riding to Baltimore Memorial Hospital in the ambulance, he knew his throwing arm and shoulder were broken. Upon arrival he was immediately X-rayed and diagnosed with a fracture of the right elbow and shoulder. Three days later Chad was released and was told he would never play football again.

The school discovered Chad had been sneaking out with Carl and restricted them to quarters for the next ninety days. Chad was able to leave for medical and therapy visits while Carl just drove himself crazy waiting for the time to elapse. The girls were prohibited from visiting them, and the time just dragged. When the ninety days ended, Chad decided to move on. The injury, loss of school time, and not being able to play again were the reasons for his decision.

During his waiting days his cousin Jeb Braden had reached out to Chad. He was an attaché to naval intelligence located in Alexandria, Virginia, and he invited Chad to live with him in his two-bedroom condo. Jeb's girlfriend, Marcy, lived there also, and he made a point of warning Chad not to interfere with their relationship.

"Otherwise you're welcome, and I'll get you in as an investigator trainee."

Chad was jubilant but sad about leaving Sherry and the good sexual times. They met for dinner, and Chad told Sherry of his new plans.

She grew upset and bolted from the table in tears. He ran after her but could not convince her to calm down and listen to him.

She said, "All I ever was to you was a sex toy. It's now obvious that you never loved me. I gave you my body, and you just get rid of me. I don't ever want to see you again. Don't try to call me because we're done forever." Sherry ran to her mother's Mercedes and took off.

The very next day he was in Virginia and starting a new chapter in his life. Jeb was six years his senior but looked much older. He had a wrinkled face and forehead, indicating his years of work had already affected him. Jeb was a nerd but was a perfect host.

When Jeb left the apartment to run an errand, Marcy immediately came on to Chad. Her body was the best part of her because she definitely was not a looker. She kept kneading his arm while they were talking and reminded Chad that she was only down the hall. As she walked away, her ass was shaking like a ship in turbulent waters.

Chad said to himself, "I can't stay here without getting a piece of that action. Maybe I need to find another place to crash."

When they entered the naval building, Jeb turned to him and said, "Don't fuck up. This could be a lifetime career for you, if you handle it right. I'm going to bring you to HR and leave you there. I'll see you later."

HR had him complete his papers and brought him to meet Jack Sutters. His new boss was about ten years older than Chad and was a little taller than a dwarf. He was built close to the ground, but his stature obviously did not bother him.

Jack said to Chad, "You're going to be my trainee, and I expect you not to make any decisions until you consult me. What you're going to be doing is reading shore police reports from all our naval facilities. If you sense anything is troublesome, criminal, or suspicious, point it out to me. I'll then show you how to follow up."

"That's all I have to do to get started?"

"Yes." Sutters neglected to tell him that the stack of reports was only for one day.

His desk was in a six-by-six cubicle with a telephone line and fax machine. There was a line of cubicles, but he couldn't see anyone else, although he heard voices. Only when he got up to use the men's room was he able to see other people.

So the first day began with meaningless reports and a lot of boredom. He then began to wonder if he had done the right thing. That feeling only lasted for the next couple of days. He came upon a report about a sailor aboard the ship *USS Johnson* who had stabbed a fellow sailor fifteen times and then was apprehended. The ship's doctor classified the attack as the work of a mental breakdown with no criminal intent. He took the report to Sutters who said, "Let's go see Lt. Brigida."

They ventured to the fifth floor that had a series of offices like the cubicles on the second floor. Lt. Brigida turned out to be Nellie Brigida, a five foot eight blonde in a navy uniform wearing black horn-rimmed glasses.

Chad said to himself, "She's about five years older than me, but it's hard to tell what she really looks like since the uniform doesn't do her body justice."

He and Sutters shared the report with her, and after five minutes of a one-sided conversation, Nellie said rather abruptly, "Thank you; that will be all."

It was a real drag going back to Jeb's apartment every night. The rooms were so small that every sound could be heard by the others. Jeb and Marcy's intimate adventures produced sighs, yells, and grunts that kept Chad from sleeping nights. Marcy was a real yeller, and her shouts announced her orgasms.

Additionally, during TV time she had control of the remote. That was another minus as she was addicted to soap operas and shopping channels. It was two weeks since he had started crashing at Jeb's place, and it felt like a century.

It also became apparent that Jeb could not stand having him in the apartment. His whole demeanor had changed, and there was no doubt in Chad's mind that his cousin thought that he had nailed Marcy. Having been so-blamed got him thinking about giving in to Marcy's sexual advances. It all came to fruition one day when he happened to come home early and she was just lounging around in her robe. Her top was open, slightly exposing her cleavage, and her legs were hanging out in a very provocative manner. She saw the glint in his eyes and immediately threw open her robe, revealing a beautiful body.

At that moment he decided to walk away. Marcy went wild. "How dare you do that to me? I'll get even with you, you prick!"

When Jeb came home, Marcy told him Chad had tried to rape her but she was able to fight him off.

Jeb went to Chad's bedroom and confronted him. "I told you not to touch her, and you promised you wouldn't. Get out. I'm getting you fired because you can't be trusted."

Chad found himself out of house and job within minutes simply because he had rebuffed Marcy. Having no place to go, he checked into the local Best Western for the night and would start looking for an apartment pronto. He had a sleepless night and was anxious to see what the situation at work would be.

He didn't have to wait long because Sutters met him at the door and said, "You're out of here, jerk." Just like that, a budding career was over.

Back at the hotel he called his brother, Pat, and told him what happened.

Pat said, "Don't make any hasty moves. Stick it out there, maybe you can find something else."

"I was thinking about going back home and maybe look into state university."

"You have some time, and if you need money, call Jamie Robbins. He can give you an advance on the trust fund. I'll say a prayer for you at Mass. Hang in there, brother."

They said good-bye, and Chad decided to take Pat's advice. Monday morning he would start looking for another job.

CHAPTER 5

C had visited three different employment agencies and was told by all that his lacking a college education was a real hindrance. They all had entry-level positions to fill such as bank clerk, post office worker, fast food management trainee, car salesman, and others, but none appealed to him. After a week, he had enough and decided to go back to Quenton.

When the new semester came about a short month away, he planned to enter state university.

But all that changed when he received a strange message at the hotel. Clary the front desk clerk said a female naval officer was by looking for him. Instead of waiting, she left a message. He opened the envelope, which stated, "Meet me tonight at nine at the Marriott bar by the water on Jefferson. I have something for you. Signed, Nellie Brigida."

He couldn't hide his anxiety and surprise when he left for this meeting. As Chad walked in, he spotted Nellie at a table by herself. She was dressed in civilian clothes: a black two-piece suit with a short skirt and high heels. Her blonde hair was long and flowing on her shoulders, and her legs were slim and exciting.

She said, "Sit down. Do you want a drink?" while waving around a martini.

He said, "I'll have a Heineken."

"I guess you're wondering why I wanted to meet with you."

"I think I figured it out—you want my body."

"Don't be a wise ass."

"Okay, why then?"

"There's trouble at Ocean Naval Academy. A big drug ring is operating there, and the administration has no clue who's behind it. We know two football players are the couriers and have been targeted. This is where you would come in. When I heard that Sutters fired you, it boggled my mind, because I thought you had all the goods to do your job.

"Anyway, it's no secret I think that Sutters is an asshole, so I immediately thought of you. This assignment is a natural fit for your help. I know you don't have any investigative experience, but I liked your work with Sutter. If you want in, this is the scenario. After the job, the navy will give you a sixteen-week boot camp, with a two-year academic course and a commission upon completion. That's if you're able to pull off this assignment."

"That sounds great, but what would I need to do?"

"Go back to the school in the new semester and be our undercover man. It's a no-brainer since you know all the football players and the school terrain."

"But I don't want to be a squealer and a spy."

"Unfortunately, that is the job. You have overnight to think about it. Call me in the morning."

All night he argued with himself as to why he should become a spy. Finally he was convinced that this may a chance for his future. He called Nellie in the morning and said yes.

She said, "Meet me at the Marriott tonight at six. I don't want anyone here to know that you're undercover on this investigation."

When he arrived at the hotel, she was sitting at the same table wearing her uniform. This time Chad thought, *She's all business, nothing else.*

Nellie said, "You're going to have to reapply to Ocean, but that shouldn't be a problem. Try to get on the football team in a nonplaying position, and then try to figure out how to get close to Kit and Ernie, the suspected drug dealers. Once you do that, use them to get information about the operation and the identity of 'Mr. Zero.' That is the name the head of the organization goes by."

"Did you say Kit and Ernie? Kit was my center, and Ernie's the equipment manager."

"Right. Try to get very close to them, because they'll lead you to the top people. At the school, act like any other student. Ask for a single room because of your injury. Tell them you have a hard time sleeping nights and don't want to keep anyone up. Look up your old girlfriends so everything appears normal. I'm your contact, and this is my private number. Memorize it and discard the paper." She handed him her card.

"Lastly, I am giving you $25,000 in cash in the event they don't renew your scholarship, and the rest is for your pay and living expenses. Don't tell anyone about this assignment, not even your brother, Pat. Your life and future depend on the success of this operation. You can't misstep on anything—it could cost you your life. Any second thoughts?"

"No."

CHAPTER 6

C had was walking across the campus on the way to Coach Glenn's office when he ran into Carl.

Carl appeared startled and said, "What are you doing here?"

"I'm back and staying at the Elm dorm in a single room. I was just on my way to see the coach about giving me a football-related job. How about you? How's it going?"

"Fine. I have to get to class." Carl left in a hurry.

The coach gave him the job of keeping track of the number of plays that each football player would have during practice and games. As he left the coach's office, he was already thinking about a starting point. He thought about hooking up with Hank "Kit" Carson and Ernie Jinks.

Kit was a six foot six brute that had the bulk of a body that served as the starting center of the team, and Ernie was the equipment manager. He was five foot four and was a weakling in comparison. The two spent a lot of time together, and he was the person known to have access to the team's drugs.

Chad called Sherry's home in Quenton and her mother answered the phone. "Chad, she left for New York City and said she has a modeling career going for her. Sherry instructed me not to give you her phone number. Sorry."

With that behind him, he turned his attention to how to get close to Kit and Ernie. He had heard that this duo would visit a bar called the Jada Club in Washington DC every Friday night.

When Chad looked them up on the following Friday and asked if he could go out with them, they made a point of asking why was he now seeking their company. He answered in a gruff voice, "I'm tired of being alone. Any problem with that?"

That very same night they went to the Jada. It was a strange place wherein the clientele were all men. But it wasn't a gay bar, just a place where guys could hang out. The bartenders were a set of redheaded twins dressed in men's clothing and had the appearance of being lesbians—dressed in men's clothing with very short, butch haircuts.

Upon entering, Kit and Ernie went right over to the area near the old-fashioned and outdated jukebox. Craig Betts, Bob Tanto, and Peter McKay, also students, were sitting there drinking and smoking. They did not look too happy to see Chad but nevertheless accepted him into their circle and spent the night drinking shots of Jack Daniels with a beer chaser. All night long they were shooting the breeze until closing time at about three in the morning.

The same get-together took place for the next three weeks without any mention of drugs. Finally, on the fourth Friday, Kit and Ernie took him to this remote little red house on the outskirts of College Town, Maryland. It became obvious that the first three weeks had been a test, and now they were going to share their dark secret with him.

The other guys were already there. Seeing him, they came over and shook his hand.

Craig said, "Welcome to the little red house where all the action is."

Chad looked around and was surprised at how bad the interior looked. It had plastic and wooden crates instead of chairs, walls painted blood-red, and wooden floors showered with black paint in a completely haphazard manner.

Chad said, "Where are the girls?"

Kit said, "Hold on, cowboy, not so fast. Look around first; you might see something you like."

He went into a couple of rooms and saw girls and guys making out or smoking pot. Some were visiting the john, feeding their cocaine problem. When he got back to the living room, the guys were smoking pot. Ernie gave him a joint, and Chad had to smoke it or blow his cover. Having never experienced the drug, it hit him like a brick shithouse. He felt that he was in la-la land and couldn't speak because his mouth felt like it had been doused with Novocain. From the corner of his eye, he thought that he saw Carl and Jeri leave the house.

Then again, it could be another illusion brought on by the weed, because Jeri would not permit herself to be included in the action and perversion of the little red house.

After a couple of similar visits to the house and watching the whole operation, he concluded that they were not only using but bringing it back to campus. The big break occurred when Kit told him they would be going to a new meeting place. It was a repair garage for sailboats on campus, located near the water and isolated from other buildings.

The usual guys were there, plus seven freshman who apparently were good customers.

One said to Kit, "Why did you bring him here?"

Kit answered, "He's okay," and proceeded to hand out drugs. He turned to Chad and said, "Collect the cash, and let's split."

The next day Chad contacted Nellie and told her where the activity was taking place. She instructed him to find out who Mr. Zero was and said, "We'll raid the boathouse two Fridays from now. That will give you time to question Kit and Ernie. During the raid, resist arrest vocally and physically. That will give us the chance to separate you from the others."

Chad dropped subtle questions with Kit about Mr. Zero's identity, but he wouldn't bite.

He did the same with Ernie, who said, "Don't ask me those questions." He sensed Ernie had become somewhat suspicious, while Kit, who was not as sharp as Ernie, shrugged it off.

During the two weeks, they kept the same schedule, visiting the bar and boathouse plus a couple of other stops, when Kit would have Chad wait in the car.

Finally, the raid took place. It was around ten at night, and about fifteen people were in the boathouse. Kit and Ernie were there, as well as five regulars and eight freshman who happened to be there to buy drugs.

The shore police moved in fast and pinned everyone against the wall, including Chad. Ernie was next to him. The SP turned his back in order to give an instruction, and Ernie took advantage of the movement to pull out a gun and point it at Chad's head.

Ernie then yelled, "I'm leaving with this snitch who I never trusted. Don't try to stop me—otherwise he's a dead man."

Ernie took Chad to the back of the building and said, "Mr. Zero was right. You're a fucking snitch. Don't worry. I'm not going to kill you, but you'd better start looking over your shoulder." He then hit him twice in the forehead with the butt of the pistol and took off.

Chad was bleeding profusely. He got up and staggered to the front of the building and fainted.

The shore police then found him and took him to nearby St. Luke's Hospital. He was to remain there for three weeks suffering from severe lacerations, concussion, and painful headaches. These headaches would plague him for the rest of his life.

CHAPTER 7

They spent hours searching the vast campus and could not find Ernie. The shore police questioned Kit for information of his partner's whereabouts, but he clammed up. The school provided Ernie's parents' address in Newark, Delaware, some sixty miles away. The next morning two shore detectives plus three local cops went to the house.

Seated on the steps was an old white-haired man with a beard who appeared to be waiting for them. "If you want Ernie, he's inside the house and is unarmed. You can take him; we didn't raise that boy to be a criminal." With that, he called Ernie to come out.

They cuffed him and left without any further problems from their prisoner. The grandfather chose not to speak or look at his grandson, who had shamed the family beyond their belief and expectations. He was a wounded man.

When asked why he did such a stupid act of escaping and assault, he mumbled the stock response: "I want a lawyer."

The next day his appointed defender spoke to the JAG attorney, who made an offer to both Ernie and Kit. "Give up Mr. Zero and you both can walk without any jail time."

They both refused and ended up with five-year sentences. All the other midshipmen who were present at the boathouse during the raid were expelled.

What Chad and the authorities didn't know was that Carl was Mr. Zero's right-hand man. He had become suspicious of Chad and had warned Ernie and Kit. Kit never bought into what he was saying about Chad.

However, Ernie did. Carl had seen the new Chad and surmised something was up. His speculations proved to be right, and Chad had become a target.

Carl had another beef with Chad: he didn't like the way he looked at Jeri. He continually undressed her with his eyes. It became so uncomfortable that he was eliminated from their circle, which only added to the hatred. Chad accepted becoming an outcast because he knew it was the truth. He just couldn't help himself when it came to Jeri.

The next three years were uneventful for Chad, other than finishing boot camp and intelligence school. Upon graduation he was given the rank of ensign and assigned to Nellie Brigida's unit. She had asked for him, and it was obvious there was some chemistry there.

His cousin Jeb, who worked in the same building, made a point of stopping by and apologizing to Chad. He conceded that Marcy had made the whole thing up about his rape attempt. She was gone from his life, and he wanted to make amends. Chad accepted Jeb's apology but really didn't have too much to do with him thereafter.

Pat was ordained and became a parishioner priest in residence at the cathedral in Baltimore.

The church was a beautiful structure built with a gothic architecture pattern after the churches in Europe. His brother would later become elevated to pastor of Saint Mary's and monsignor of this parish comprised of ten thousand practicing Catholics.

Meanwhile, he had learned that Carl, after graduation from Ocean Academy, had been assigned to a naval base in Naples, Italy. Jeri had joined Carl, and they were married in Rome at a Vatican chapel. Jeri's family paid for Father Pat to attend and perform the ceremony. It was Pat who gave him the news and couldn't understand why Chad had not been invited. Chad had no comment.

CHAPTER 8

Two years later Chad and Pat were invited to the White House. President Garrett had just been elected to a first term and was appointing Jamie Robbins, Jeri's father, as the US ambassador to the country of Gamba in the Middle East. Gamba was a semi-democracy bolstered by a strong economy because of its abundance of oil. The major oil wells were in the north and close in proximity to Karner, run by a dictatorship governed with an iron hand and oblivious of the human rights of its inhabitants. Jamie had been paramount in the president's campaign and was now being rewarded.

Father Pat could not make the reception, so Chad was there alone. He was overwhelmed by the White House as he had never been there before. The reception was being held in a room called the Kennedy Hall. There were about one hundred people milling about and a group of others standing by a corner bar. Carl and Jeri were in that group, engrossed in a conversation with an impeccably dressed older man who was accompanied by a gorgeous silver-haired lady.

Carl noticed Chad and motioned for him to come over. Jeri and Carl welcomed him warmly, to his surprise. He was then introduced to Carl's uncle, Congressman George Koski, who was his mother's brother. He was the congressional representative from the Polish district in Chicago and also the owner-publisher of the *Polish Tribune*. The lady was his wife, Sylvia. George had deserted his party and delivered the Polish vote for the newly elected Republican president.

The man was an arrogant person who kept bragging loudly, "See my friend Jamie Robbins? I made him the ambassador."

Sylvia, who appeared to be very shy, kept her distance from her husband and appeared embarrassed by his behavior.

While they were making small talk, Jeri took everyone by surprise when she announced she was pregnant and very happy about it. Actually, no one could have surmised as she was dressed in an elegant designer gown with a sexy low cleavage. She looked radiant and wholesome. This news complicated Chad's feelings and compounded the situation with Jeri ever so more. Fifteen minutes later, Chad said good night and left, not knowing when he would ever see her again.

To his amazement Jeri took him aside and whispered, "I'll miss you, dear Chad."

He didn't know what to make of that and chose not to respond.

Three months later he was told that Carl and Jeri were now stationed at the ambassador's embassy. Carl was the liaison officer and commander of the marines attached to the embassy. Jeri's mom, Ginny, was suffering from the early stages of MS and welcomed her daughter's presence and help. Jeri had lost the baby but physically was sound. On the other hand, Chad felt bad for her but was selfishly relieved that she was not a mother yet. In his mind he thought there might be still a chance for him, however slight.

Chad had an apartment in Alexandria, Virginia, and out of sheer boredom, started to explore for a weekend getaway. He was successful in finding Pocomoke, Maryland, on the southern tip of the Oceanside. It was a quaint seashore resort with one-family ranches built about five hundred feet from the shoreline. Other than a few restaurants, a general store, a movie house, and two bed-and-breakfast boarding homes, there was very little to disturb the peace. Once discovered, Chad began to spend every weekend at one of the boarding homes and enjoying the small public beach.

Chad was at the general store when he ran into an old professor from the academy, Rear Admiral Chancy. He said they'd had a summer home for years at Pocomoke, and upon retirement they had moved here permanently. The admiral invited him for dinner.

Upon arriving, Chad was amazed at the sprawling house by the water's edge. Mrs. Chancy was a distinguished writer of spy novels, and their way of life was proof of her success. She was very much interested in Chad because of his work in Intelligence. The woman was twenty years younger than her husband and was extremely attractive. They had twin sons who had graduated from the academy and were now stationed in Hawaii. Oddly enough, there was not too much talk about them in the Chancy household.

CHAPTER 9

Not long after the Chancys asked Chad to stay in their house whenever he came down for the weekend. Without failure, he was given their son Robbie's room. They seemed to follow a set routine. First dinner, then a game of chess with the admiral, and then bed at ten. He said he was an earlier riser. Mrs. Chancy would then entertain Chad by discussing her spy book ideas. Together they worked on the plot and most times would engage in political conversations. Unlike her husband, she was an ultra-liberal and very outspoken about the failures of American society.

She had asked Chad to call her Della and always preached a vegetarian diet and exercise. Her regimen consisted of walking five miles a day. This accounted for her great youthful shape at age fifty-two. Many times Chad felt she was coming on to him, but he was hesitant about making a move. However, he wasn't surprised when one night, after a couple of drinks, the situation became more intense. Around eleven, the admiral was fast asleep. She grabbed Chad's hand and brought him into the den.

She put her body up against him and kissed him rather strongly. "Chad, I want you to make love to me."

"I can't do that because of the admiral."

"Don't be silly. He doesn't care. Why do you think he leaves us alone all the time? He expects it will happen. Besides, he hasn't been able to deliver for quite some time."

Chad felt very uncomfortable, and although he was enthralled by her shapely body, he said, "I'm sorry, but I can't."

Della then backed off and changed the subject to her new book.

Chad was totally surprised when she started to give him an outline of her latest work. The main character was a young naval officer who worked in the Intelligence department. This officer betrays his country by sharing nuclear submarine secret details of construction with the Russian government. He told her she should not have used him as the traitor and felt that it would come back to haunt him.

Della passed his complaint off rather easily by saying, "It's only a fictitious novel."

A few weeks later Della said to him, "My niece Mary lives five miles from here and would like to take you to a party next weekend. Is it okay?"

"That's very nice of her, and of course I'd be glad to go."

"Good. I'll tell her so. It's next Saturday, and she'll pick you up here at eight."

*

The week went by very fast, and on Saturday, this very pretty girl of about twenty-one drove up in a white Saab convertible. The destination was at a party in the nearby town of Livingston Park. She explained that her girlfriend was married to this yuppie and they lived in a small mansion. That was her wedding gift from her well-to-do parents. Mary did all the talking during the twenty-minute ride, and all he did was sit back and take it all in.

She explained that her girlfriend, Gert, was married to this yuppie and they lived in a semi-mansion. Gert was very sociable, but her husband paid no attention to them. He was off in another room with some business associates. Mary appeared edgy and hardily tried to mingle. This Mary was quite different from the one who couldn't stop talking moments ago. Throughout the night she kept hanging onto Chad like there was no tomorrow. Chad wanted to leave, but Mary insisted on staying three hours. She didn't want to hurt her girlfriend's feelings by leaving early.

When they left, Chad said to her, "What was that all about?"

She shocked him when she answered, "This date was a total set up. My uncle called and said someone professing to be an interested party visited them and threatened to out their sons as homosexuals unless they agree to destroy you. He told me they could never live with that disgrace and agreed to this person's demands. You were the target. I was to fake a rape by you at the party. The plan was for me to get you into a bedroom and yell rape. I was on the verge of doing it several times but could never bring myself to do it. Chad, you have to help them because I know they're frightened to death of what is going to happen now."

As they pulled onto their road, flames and clouds of smoke were pouring out of the Chancy home. Five fire trucks blocked the road.

Mary cried, "Chad, it's my auntie's house!"

He jumped out of the car, ran past two firemen and the big burly chief, and raced into the house. The smoke was dense, and he attempted to find Della and the admiral. Della was in the den and Chad tried to calm her. Finally he grabbed her and forcibly carried her out. She was giving him a hard time, yelling, "Find my husband!"

He could never go back in as the flames were just too high. Nothing further could be done. The paramedics took over, and the fire chief came over to speak to Chad and Mary. "We did everything we could, but my men couldn't find him because of the smoke. There's no doubt in my mind that arson was the cause. One of the neighbors saw a black Lincoln abruptly pull away from the house just minutes before the fire started."

Turning to Mary, he asked, "Where were you two, and do you know why this fire would have been set?"

Mary broke down and could not speak.

Chad said, "I think I may have been the cause," and left it at that.

Chad took Mary and Della to Nellie Brigida for protection. The plan was that after the admiral's funeral, they both will be relocated and given new identities. Intelligence took over the investigation and interviewed Kit and Ernie in jail.

Both said they had nothing to do with the fire, and one added he hoped "that fucking snitch gets his someday soon."

Unfortunately, a leak from the investigation released the information that the sons were gay and put their navy careers in jeopardy. Further, it was never made known that Chad was the real target.

There was a largely attended memorial at the academy. The sons gave stirring eulogies for their decorated dad. Chad was totally ignored by Della and her family. In fact, one of the sons approached Chad and asked him to leave.

Chad went over to Della and extended his hand. She took it and said, "I hope I never see you again. You caused my husband's death and disgraced my sons. I have to lead a different life because of you."

He never went back to Pocomoke City and was ordered by his superiors to closely watch what was going on around him. The decision was made to send him on assignment to Buenos Aires, far from whomever was trying to harm him. Chad now seriously began to look over his shoulder and worried about what was next.

CHAPTER 10

C had was now the liaison officer to special services and reported to Commander Richards at the Costa Naval Base in Buenos Aires. His cover included arranging entertainment, publicity, morale building, etc. The real mission was to investigate a sexual harassment epidemic among the female officers who ran the administration of the base. There had been anonymous accusations of Commander Richards as the predator.

Upon his arrival, Chad checked in with Richards. He was old navy and demanded that everyone march to his drum beat. The redness of his face hinted that he was a drinker.

He said, "Son, you have a very easy job. I've been in the navy for thirty years and never got a free pass with an assignment like yours."

"Commander, I'm here because headquarters thought you needed a specialist like myself."

"Don't get me wrong, son. I'm only venting."

Chad sensed Richards would be trouble.

Back at Intelligence, they had hatched a plan for Chad to try to find the female officer who was making these accusations. He was to get friendly with her and use her in the investigation. It was presumed that would be the best overall strategy. Chad was also advised to form a relationship with the commander and possibly gather some incriminating information to solidify the case against him.

When Chad spotted Lt. Maria Sposa at the nearby Marriott Hotel, she was wearing a short miniskirt that advertised the whole package. She was a dark-haired and tan-skinned beauty.

Maria was eating alone. Chad sensed that she might be the accuser and went over to her table. He introduced himself and asked if he could join her. She nodded and invited him to sit. She stated that every Friday she would come by the hotel for dinner. Later, her uncle John, who had a large ranch in Verde, would pick her up, and she would spend the weekend with her cousins Netta and Rosa. Maria then acknowledged how lucky she was to have family near her assignment.

Chad broke her pace by asking what school she attended in order to get her commission.

"The Coast Guard Academy." Just then Uncle John showed up, and they left in somewhat of a hurry.

Chad was really interested in finding out more about her, so he made a date to meet her again at the Marriott. After two vodka martinis, she really opened up. "I was twelve years old when my parents died in a private plane crash. They were traveling from Newport, Rhode Island, where we lived, to her sister's house in Chapel Hill, North Carolina. I was left at home with my nanny. The small plane collided with a larger plane on the ground at Chapel Hill, and an explosion took their lives. I went to live with my aunt and uncle until they sent me to an all-girls school in Springfield, Mass. From there I went to the Coast Guard Academy."

She said that she was most comfortable at her aunt Mae's house but had to leave because of her cousin Raymond molesting her. He was sixteen at the time, and she was thirteen. It started one night when her aunt and uncle were out for the night.

Raymond came into her room and said, "Take your clothes off. You've been teasing me, and now it's time to give it up."

Maria said, "But I'm your cousin and I don't want to have sex with you."

That didn't work, and he forced her down, stealing her virginity. He continued to abuse her, and she couldn't complain because she had nowhere else to go. At that time she was unaware that Uncle John existed.

Her secret became known to the family when one of her schoolmates visiting found a condom in her bedroom. Jessie teased Maria, and she broke down, telling her all. Jessie told her mother, who in turn told Maria's aunt Mae. The next day Aunt Mae and Uncle Neil said, "We're sending you to an all-girls school up north. We now recognize that Raymond is very sick and needs help. Believe us that this is for your protection."

Maria told Chad, "They were just getting rid of me so Raymond would not to have to face the music."

Her next years were uneventful, except she was plagued with nightmares. Eventually she was able to forget and went on to the Coast Guard Academy, where she finished with a business administration degree. She had requested Buenos Aires as her first assignment because of her family research that resulted in discovering Uncle John.

Maria then turned to him and said, "I know who you are and what you are here for. You see, I sent headquarters anonymous letters about the sexual harassments. Before I go any further, I need a promise from your headquarters that upon conviction of Richards of any charges, they will take me out of here and put me in intelligence school. I want a new career. Can you contact headquarters and get their assurance?"

"I'll see what can be done." Chad left in a very confused state.

CHAPTER 11

Lt. Brigida discussed Maria with Chad and said, "If we're successful in getting Richards, we'll grant her requests." Chad met with Maria and shared the answer from Nellie. She agreed to the ground rules and promised to tell him all.

Two days later Chad and Maria met and discussed a strategy. Chad would get close to Richards and try to come up with any evidence. Maria would meet with the other females, Sue Rheiner and Jane Persey. She would not even attempt to meet with Alice Grant because they really never got along. Next they planned that Maria would meet with Sue and Jane for separate weekends at Uncle John's house.

Maria looked Chad directly in the eyes and said, "I'm scared, so please make sure nothing happens to me."

Chad answered, "You'll be okay."

Maria then opened up and told Chad of her experiences with Commander Richards. "I was on the base about three weeks when he ordered me to report to his office. He talked to me about the supply station and then invited me to the club for dinner. I felt compelled to go because he was my superior. We sat in a corner booth, and he talked about his failed marriage. He kept stroking my arm and at least three times brushed my breast. Another time I felt his hand on my thigh, and when I moved, he withdrew his hand. I couldn't tell whether it was intentional or from the drinks. When it was time to leave, I could not help noticing that he had an erection. But I couldn't leave him alone because he was too drunk, or so I thought.

"I brought him back to his apartment and went inside to help him. That was my mistake, as he immediately pounced on me. I was able to fight him off and run for the door. He tried to stop me, but I was able to avoid him. The next day Commander Richards called me and apologized for his actions. He said he'd never done anything like that before and wanted it to end there. Later that day, he sent me a class-A pass by special courier."

Chad said, "I don't think that's enough to proceed with formal charges. We'll need corroborating testimony. Maybe you can get it from others who have had a similar experience with the commander. Meanwhile, I'm going to try to socialize with him and see what I can develop to support your case."

The next night he met Richards at the officers club and was surprised at how mild mannered Richards was. Drinks and dinner became a frequent occasion for the two, and Chad was now forming a different opinion of the man. He didn't drink much and never mentioned women.

Chad started to casually talk to the navy personnel who ran the officers club. None gave him anything to work with. In fact, it was the opposite. They never saw him drunk or with a woman at the club. Chad thought something was wrong with this picture, so he decided to confront Maria with his observations.

She said, "He must be on to you. Next weekend I'll be meeting with Sue. I'll let you know what she has to say."

At their next dinner, Commander Richards told Chad, "I checked up on you and know you are with headquarters intelligence unit. I became suspicious when you started to spend time with me and by your friendship with Lt. Maria Sposa. I don't know what's going on, but let me tell you, the one you should be investigating is Maria and her cousin Carlo."

"What does he have to do with the navy?"

"Plenty! Maria recommended him as the only civilian employee at the base supply station. He's been there for months and works under Lt. Sposa in administration. However, it appears that he is also extremely tight with Seaman Pat Trento. Together they run the day-to-day operation. There have been rumors that equipment and arms are unaccounted for. I've asked HQ for an audit, but as of now I have not received an answer."

When Chad left, he started to reason as to whether Maria might be creating a smoke screen trying to get rid of Richards. This would give Carlo and Trento a clear path to do whatever they wanted at supply. He decided to call Nellie and told her they might be wrong about Richards and maybe Maria is setting up HQ. It was conceivable because all the information was coming from one direction: Maria.

After a long discussion, Nellie came up with a plan to test Maria, Carlo, and Trento. She said, "Suppose we advise Richards and Maria that a shipment of missiles are being sent to the base for storage. We would make sure the missiles are ineffective and have undetected tracking devices. The date of delivery will be ten days from today. Let's see what happens then. Meanwhile, proceed with the impression that you are pursuing Richards. Keep pressing Maria about getting the corroborating testimony from Sue and Jane. It will be interesting to see if she will be able to produce them, unless they're part of a conspiracy. Don't let Richards in on the plan, because the agency will have to prosecute him if Maria is legit. You'll be furnished with a monitor that will be activated if the missiles are moved. If that happens, advise the shore police. Watch your back, and keep in contact."

CHAPTER 12

On Monday morning Chad asked Maria how she made out this past weekend with Sue. She answered that Sue never came and that she backed out at the last minute. Supposedly she would try to make it next weekend.

Meanwhile, that didn't stop Chad from having dinner with Richards. His behavior was reflective of an innocent person, and Chad felt uneasy about investigating him. Sometime later that week, a memorandum went out to the supply station and Richards informing them the missiles would be arriving shortly. Later that day, Richards told Chad about the delivery and said he was concerned about the safekeeping of the weapons. This delivery was by far the biggest to ever arrive at the base.

Richards said, "The reason I'm telling you this is because I need your help. I don't know what you're doing here, but I'm glad you are here. I have a feeling that Carlo, Trento, and Maria are going to do something that will jeopardize the navy's use of these weapons."

Chad then responded without ever admitting to his being with intelligence. "I'll try to monitor their activities and keep you informed." However, because of certain unexplained reservations, he had second thoughts about informing the commander about the expected attempt when it would come.

About a week later Chad was about to jump into the shower when the monitor alarm went off. He immediately studied the tracking direction and called the shore police. They wouldn't respond to him because they didn't know him, and they needed an order from the base commander to go that far off site. That meant he had to call the commander.

Richards said, "Meet me at the shore police headquarters, and bring the tracking device. I'm sure they'll let us go along on the raid."

Fifteen minutes later Chad was at the shore police headquarters. Commander Richards was already there. They all looked at the device. Chad concluded that the destination was north of the base and in the direction of Verde, where Uncle John's ranch was. When asked how he knew that, he said it was because Maria had brought him there once.

The caravan consisted of six black Jeeps carrying two police officers each and a command car. Captain Keller was in charge of the raid, and he directed Commander Richards and Chad to ride with him.

At the ranch, a large truck was parked next to an old gray barn. Some police had already surrounded the house, and the rest went to the barn area. Carlo and Trento were directing the ranch hands to bring the ten missiles into the empty barn area. Both men were totally engrossed and never even saw the shore police ganging up on them. They surrendered without any incident. The ranch hands followed suit.

Richards and Chad were asked by the captain to wait outside as they entered the house. Again there was no fight. They brought out Uncle John, a man of seventy, his sickly wife, Nona, and Maria and Rosa. Maria wasn't saying much, and Rosa astounded everyone when she turned to Maria and called her Netta.

"Please tell them about Maria in the hidden room in the house, so they can get her out here."

With that, the police searched the house room by room and found the hidden room below ground. In it they found this dark-haired, dark-complexioned young woman. When asked her name, she responded, "Lt. Maria Sposa."

The real Maria was the spitting image of her cousin Netta, who was the fake Maria. She was in decent shape although she had been kept a prisoner since her arrival. Maria rode with them in the command car and told them what happened. Once she arrived in Buenos Aires, she was excited to see her relatives. Instead of reporting to the base, she got a cab to take her to Uncle John's house. Once there, she met Uncle John, his wife, Nona, cousin Netta, her boyfriend, Carlo, and Rosa. Uncle John could not believe how much Maria looked like Netta and immediately took advantage of the similarity. First, he wanted to know if anyone at the base had seen Maria, and when she said no, he ordered Netta to pose as Maria. Netta, who was a college grad majoring in business administration, agreed rather willingly.

The real Maria was placed in a hidden room below ground level, and Uncle John promised her that she would be safe from any harm. He was a portly and bitter old man who became greedy as his years advanced. He had become one of the richest arms dealers in the area, and now utilizing his niece's true identity, he was looking to add to his fortune. The missile theft was the height of his objective.

Maria was kept comfortable but isolated from the rest of the family. According to Maria, Uncle John gave her the option of joining their business or kept apart and hidden until they figured out what to do with her. That caused her great concern. Her only social moment was when young Rosa would visit her in the room. During meal times she ate with the family but wasn't allowed to speak. Maria was trying to devise a plan of escape until Rosa told her that she thought the navy was getting closer to them. Then it happened! Uncle John, Netta, and Carlo were captured by the local police for prosecution, and Seaman Trento was taken into custody by the shore police. Maria was taken to the base hospital for overnight observation.

The next day Chad visited her and was pleased to see that she was In good physical and mental condition. She was dressed in her navy whites and was ready to be discharged from the hospital. He was amazed at how strong she was, and most of all he took in her great looks and legs. Chad felt that familiar tingle and knew they were going to become a couple.

Maria had the same feeling and sensed Chad would make sure that they would be together. She utilized the moment to ask Chad about getting her out of Buenos Aires to stateside and said, "I know we just met, but I want to be close to you. Please talk to your superior about getting me into headquarters.

There was no way Chad could say no, and he relished the moment. He said he would talk to Lt. Brigida and provide a response shortly.

The next day both he and Maria received orders to come back to Virginia and report to headquarters. They took a commercial flight, occupying two first class seats. Once aboard they were given food and wine of their choice. They consumed several glasses and were feeling very loose and giddy. She held his hand for a long time and then, without any warning, leaned over and kissed him passionately on the lips. Chad responded and now was ready for a new woman in his life.

CHAPTER 13

Things weren't going so well at headquarters. Nellie was very jealous of Chad's relationship with Maria and did a lot to keep them apart. Chad and Maria would see each other every weekend and any other chance they could fit in. But other than holding hands and kissing, there was no lovemaking, and this frustrated him to no end. There seemed to be a reluctance on her part whenever he tried to consummate their relationship.

Chad didn't know what to make of it and finally exploded one night. "What is it with you? Do you want me? If not, I'm not going to waste my time."

Maria stared to cry. "Chad, I want you, but give me some time. I'm having problems and am finding it hard to go all the way."

Chad accepted that, and they continued to see each other.

They kept observing this black Lincoln Town Car following them whenever they were out. A couple of times they spotted the driver sitting in the restaurants they frequented. On one occasion he was in the lobby of a movie theater in Georgetown. Chad approached and asked him, "Are you following us and why?"

He said in perfect English, "Sorry, I don't speak English," and abruptly left. They never saw him after that encounter.

Meanwhile, Nellie was throwing some strong hints about seeing Chad on a social and personal level. She arranged to meet him for drinks at the Hilton bar. He could not help noticing how sexy she looked standing in a corner of the bar. She was in a short skirt dress with a tight-fitting sweater that emphasized her curves and made her a poster figure for any magazine.

Like a chump, he went up to her and planted a kiss on her cheek. For the next couple of hours he managed to mention Maria about ten times and that they were a couple. Anyone except Chad could see that Nellie wasn't too thrilled about that subject matter. They left that night on a cordial note.

The next morning Nellie retaliated by sending Maria to an administrative office in Baltimore and Chad to the navy's field office in London that they shared with the Brits. He now was a bench jockey with a mission to monitor all the intelligence from the Middle East. The headquarters was located on Edge Street in an old office building that had been completely renovated. There were three floors of cubicles measuring ten by ten and separated by a thin wall. Out of the twenty-two operatives at the location, two were Americans.

When he reported, they walked him through to his office and introduced him to his next-door neighbor, Derek Hanson. He was about forty-two, friendly, and accommodating. "Chad, your apartment is not in the best of sections, but the good news is it's only three long blocks from here. If you want, we can leave now and I'll take you there."

The apartment was very cozy and comfortable but lacking in much furniture and a TV. Chad was told that if he wanted to upgrade, he would have to offset the cost using his own money.

In his cubicle was a teletype machine that advised him of the different illegal activities of navy and marine personnel stationed in the Middle East. It didn't take him long to settle in, and Derek made it much easier for him to become accustomed to the daily operation. He had been told there had not been too much activity in the past few months and he could not expect too much more. For some time all he had been working on were simple mundane matters. This all changed overnight when a string of heroin and cocaine arrests emerged from the US embassies in his sector. Batches of Marines, along with embassy employees, were being detained at an alarming rate. The situation required an intensive investigation.

Chad contacted his superior at the office, Captain Ted Wilkes, who said, "You need help on this. Can you give me the name of another agent?"

He recommended his love, Maria.

Wilkes said, "She maybe too new—do you have anyone else in mind?

"Maria is a quick study and a strong person, so please reconsider."

One week later Chad was climbing the back stairs to his office when an explosion rocked the building. The impact threw him against a steel door that caused a cut on his forehead and right arm. He picked himself up and ran the rest of the way to his cubicle, which had been blasted to pieces.

He saw Derek Hanson lying prone on the floor covered with furniture and debris. He was bleeding from his nose and ears and had a serious laceration to his stomach. Chad was able to extricate him, but he was in very bad shape.

Derek moaned. "I don't want to die." He was placed on a stretcher and put into the ambulance. Chad was with him when he lapsed into an unconscious state and died shortly thereafter.

Chad possessed plenty of guilt knowing the bomb was meant for him. He kept thinking about the wife and three young girls who would never see and hold Derek again. It was a repeat of what had happened in Maryland—someone died because he was the real target. The whole office knew Derek died because of the "Yankee." Again, he was persona non grata at the funeral. Very few people took the time to talk to him, and the widow was rather cold to him.

In the investigation of the bombing, it became apparent that a Karner tourist group was passing the building at the time of the blast. The group was a bunch of high school kids supervised by six adults. They were found to be housed at the Nelson House located at Trinity Square. The agency sent a task force to the rooms and interviewed everyone in the group. Each interview took about twenty minutes. At the end, the exchange of information produced two possible suspects. Several of the students saw two men dressed as policemen running from the building seconds before the explosion. They were wearing sneakers and yelling to each other in a foreign tongue.

The investigators had felt it was too much of a coincidence that this group was right there when the bomb went off. It was their gut instinct that they were operating as a cover for the bombers. Two days later the office received a call from the "Remember Me" organization claiming responsibility for the attack.

Chad did not buy it and still considered himself the target. That feeling was confirmed when he received an anonymous note reading, "Sorry we missed you, but your time will come." It was signed, "Nobody."

Chad's security became a major concern for the agency, so his superiors decided to place him in the living quarters in the basement under guard. Meanwhile, the forensic experts had no luck in matching the fragments to a particular type of bomb. It was a puzzle.

CHAPTER 14

Captain Wilkes visited Chad and told him Nellie Brigida would be joining the team in London. Chad asked about Maria and was informed that she had suffered a mental breakdown. She was presently hospitalized at the Grove City Psychiatric Hospital, a satellite of Walter Reed, receiving treatment. Upon hearing that bad news, he wondered what was his future with Maria was now going forward.

When Nellie arrived, she had disturbing news for him. "I have a classified message for you. The White House has received two calls from your old friend, Ambassador Robbins, stating there was trouble at the embassy in Gamba. It seems that valuable and classified documents were stolen, and he could not account for their disappearance. He went on to say that his son-in-law, Carl Tracka, who was the commander of the Marine Guard, was a prime suspect. Maria and I had met his uncle, Congressman George Koski, at a naval women's luncheon in Washington. He asked about you, and we filled him in. He proceeded to tell us how his nephew Carl was your roommate at Ocean Academy. When the Robbins calls came in, I was assigned the task of approaching the congressman about some other business but with the intent of finding out if he knew about the activities at the embassy. I got nowhere."

A few days later, the whole situation at the Gamba embassy was referred to the London field office for further investigation. Captain Wilkes called a meeting for the three of them. He said the ambassador was shaky, panicky, and feared for their lives. A plan was unfolded to get to the bottom of the thefts and rescue the family from the grips of their enemies.

It was determined that Nellie would replace Carl's adjutant assistant.

Before leaving the office, Nellie said she was going to make a point of trying to get close to Carl and his wife to find out the real story.

Captain Wilkes was concerned about Nellie's safety and pulled Chad aside. "You know she's never been on a field assignment. Do you know whether she'll be able to handle it? Because things may be so bad that she would be stepping into a line of fire."

Chad assured him that Nellie was the right person as Carl would be unsuspecting of her. The overall plan was to have Chad replace Nellie after one month of service. Chad would arrive a week before the transition to familiarize himself to his new duty.

The night before she left, Nellie came to Chad's basement apartment. Chad sensed that she was now going to discard her standoffish exterior. He approached her and began to unbutton her blouse.

She pushed him away and said, sobbing, "I can't do this, although I want to very much. I am confused because of my sexual experience with Gwen, another female officer at headquarters. It started one night when she was visiting me at my apartment. I wanted to take a fast shower and she jumped right in. I was soaping myself when she began to play with every part of my body. I just gave in. I think that I got into sex with Gwen because I thought you were into Maria and I had no chance at all with you. The affair went on for about six months, and I broke off with her just before my coming to London. I have feelings for you but can't do anything about it because my head is all screwed up."

Chad felt let down because she had teased him from the outset and always was cool to any sexual advance by him. But more disturbing was her confession to an affair with another woman. He then turned his back on her and began to walk into another room.

She said, "I was hoping you would understand."

Chad turned completely around and pointed to the door.

CHAPTER 15

A week later Nellie called and acted like nothing had occurred between them. She said that Carl was nice to her but kept her from seeing the ambassador, his wife, and Jeri. "It is like they are under house arrest and restricted to their quarters. I don't think Carl is fooled and probably thinks something's up. My big problem is that I am afraid of the Marines, especially Sgt. Curtis Perry. He ignores my orders, and last night he actually pushed me hard. Moments later he said it was an accident. Chad, I'm afraid for all of us here."

Nellie continued to call, but Chad could not help being cold with her. It was totally unbelievable that Carl and Hadi, the head housekeeper, were keeping her from seeing the ambassador.

"Chad, this fellow Hadi is always having conversations with Carl and Sgt. Perry. They go off by themselves in deep talk and give off the impression that they are plotting something.'"

He said, "Maybe you should follow them some night."

Nellie thought it was too early in the operation. Right then Chad realized Nellie was scared and needed help.

Chad called Captain Wilkes the next day and requested to go to the embassy ahead of schedule. He described his conversations with Nellie and how she was falling apart. The captain was a tall, muscular, good-looking guy with a laid-back disposition. He was known for his ability to act in a crisis situation.

Without hesitation, he said, "You'd better get out there soon and send Nellie back here. But before you go, I received further bad news today from the states. Maria disappeared from the hospital three days ago and cannot be found."

Chad was dumbstruck as he never considered that she was in danger. He hoped she had chosen to leave the hospital voluntarily.

Captain Wilkes promised to keep him informed but insisted that he leave immediately to relieve Nellie.

Later that day Nellie said she was calling from an outside phone as she was fearful that they were tapping her phone. He told her what Captain Wilkes had ordered, and she sounded relieved. He would be arriving in two days.

When Chad arrived at the embassy in Gamba, Carl was waiting for him. Apparently, Nellie had told him about the change in leadership. He was very warm to Chad and that caused Chad to be perplexed. Carl had arranged for Chad to have lunch with the ambassador. This was a major surprise since Nellie had been denied contact with Robbins. He then gave Chad a tour of the complex, stopping in the administrative office and then on to a room where Chad would be able to settle in.

Ten minutes later Nellie burst into the room and ran into his arms. She began to cry. "I'm so happy that you're here. Things are so wrong. Its like the Robbinses are being held hostage, and Carl seems to be heavily involved with this man, Hadi. He appears to be the person running the whole show, with assistance from Sgt. Perry."

He then asked her if she had seen Jeri and Mrs. Robbins, and she said no. She also described how the help hardly mentioned them, as if they didn't exist.

He then filled her in about his conversation with Carl and the meeting with the ambassador.

Nellie couldn't believe it and thought there may be some trick to it.

He said, "We'll see. And where is your room, by the way?"

"Two doors from yours. I have to get back before they miss me." With that, she ran off.

He was bewildered and confused about the present situation. He kept asking himself how this could ever have happened. He was anxious to see them but first had to see for himself what the ambassador was all about.

His initial reaction when seeing Robbins was that he looked emaciated and sick. Just a few years ago he had been a tall and strapping handsome man.

"Chad, you have to help me. My wife, Jeri, and I are being held here against our will. I haven't seen Jeri in about two weeks, and my wife is locked in her room for the greater part of each day. Carl is doing this to us, and it's apparent that he is taking orders from Hadi. I know he has stolen classified documents from my private papers related to hostile Karner."

"Ambassador, what are you doing about your Marines? Have you called upon them for help?"

"No, because I don't trust them. I don't know what to do next, please help."

Chad, for the first time in his life, felt a pang of sympathy for the man.

As Chad left he was agitated about Carl's part in the takeover and betrayal to the country. His immediate reaction was to confront Carl—but that wasn't necessary since Carl appeared to be right behind the door as if eavesdropping. Carl then dragged Chad into an empty room and proceeded to relate a story that rivaled a *Star Wars* movie.

"I know we haven't been close, but here goes. Mr. Zero, the drug dealer, was my cousin, Gustave Koski, George's son. I was his main man, and Jeri knew nothing about it. I made a lot of money and was very lucky that nobody ratted me out. Most likely because they were afraid of what might happen to them. Having never been implicated, I promised myself I would never get involved again. That seemed to work until I met Hadi. Two weeks into our assignment, Hadi was hired to run the everyday details at the compound.

"Shortly thereafter I began to notice Sgt. Perry and Hadi acting like they were conspiring to do something. I was curious and followed them one night to this seemingly vacant warehouse. They went in and stayed for hours. The next day I decided to confront Sgt. Perry. He was arrogant and aloof, smiling like the cat who ate the canary. He told me I'd been spotted by a guard and that Hadi would explain what they were doing. A couple hours later, Hadi came to my room and said Jeri and her mother will be held as prisoners unless I agreed to cooperate. When I asked what would happen if I didn't, he said they would be killed. He said they would be held as hostages, and I was going to give him all secret transmissions regarding my country, Karner. I said I would give him an answer within twenty-four hours.

"Then the ordeal really began. Mrs. Robbins was pushed down the stairs and rushed to the hospital. Fortunately, she only suffered bruises. Hadi came to me and asked whether I had made my decision. From that moment on I cooperated with him. I took classified documents daily, copied them, and turned them over to Hadi. I faked the documents and stored the originals in a closest under a loose board. I know the ambassador thinks I'm in on it, but I couldn't confide in him. You're the only person I've told."

While Chad was listening to Carl, he was studying him to determine if he was being truthful. He then saw the pain in Carl's eyes and expression, and he decided to give him the benefit of doubt. "Here's the plan. We have to raid the warehouse and arrest Hadi. During the raid you need to disappear because the navy might charge you with treason. I'll report you missing in action and continue to defend your character. At least you will still be alive and making a new life rather than rotting in a prison facility."

Carl agreed and asked Chad to tell Jeri that he wasn't running out on her.

He said, "No, because you'll be compromising your whole disappearing act."

They then called Nellie and together constructed a plan of action.

The plan was to attack the next night at nine. Nellie was to handpick ten Marines who would be sworn to secrecy about the mission. Their assignment would be to guard the perimeter. Chad was to meet with the local police, because the criminal activity was within their jurisdiction. He would enter the building with them in search of Hadi and all the illegal arms and drugs.

Uppermost in Chad's mind was to eliminate Hadi and restore normalcy to the embassy. By taking out Hadi and Perry, Jeri and her mother would be freed.

He then asked Carl how he was altering the classified documents given to Hadi. He then explained that the originals were manually changed by him and passed on to Hadi.

Carl then uttered, "Chad, our next move has to be perfect as many lives are in jeopardy."

CHAPTER 16

CHAPTER 16

On the night of the raid, the moon was high and full, creating a well-lit background. There was plenty of activity at the warehouse that would cause some complications since many people were inside.

As the police and Chad broke in, people began to run. The intent was to get to the rear of the building where Carl had told them that the weapons, ammunition, and drugs were stored. They had to navigate a long and wide corridor to get there, but their progress was short lived as a contingent of armed guards pinned them down with heavy fire. The fire drew the attention of the Marines, who rushed into the building.

Carl and Nellie remained outside with two Marines.

Now with the extra firepower, they were able to advance toward the rear of the building.

The guards, recognizing they were outnumbered, disappeared into the night. As they approached the rear of the building, there was a barricade around a steel door. They removed the barricade and blew the door. Once inside the large room, they saw mountains of cash, drugs, and firearms. There was one occupant, Sgt. Perry. His throat had been slashed.

Hadi was nowhere to be found.

Chad ordered a Marine to get Carl and Nellie to come in. The marine came back shortly and said they were gone. The two Marines that were with them had been killed and a civilian told him that the two Americans, a man and woman, were forced into a truck. The civilian said Hadi was holding a machine gun against the female's head and another had a gun against Carl's head. Somehow he knew Carl's name. Chad then wondered if this man was a plant for Hadi. He said the truck took off heading northeast. Chad reasoned that they actually went to the southwest toward Karner.

With a little pressure, the man confessed that Hadi had planted him. Chad commandeered a truck and headed in the opposite direction toward Karner. He then called Captain Wilkes to have the US ambassador of Karner intercede on behalf of the two Americans kidnapped by an operative of the Karner government. The captain agreed and stated that he was sending two helicopters to assist in the search.

The search continued for hours and was discontinued at daybreak.

Upon returning to the embassy, Chad reported to the ambassador. He was distressed that his son-in-law had been abducted and wondered whether he had misjudged Carl. Chad then went to the second floor to release Mrs. Robbins and Jeri.

Jeri ran right into his arms sobbing. "I knew you would come." She was drawn, pale, and very nervous.

Mrs. Robbins was sitting in a wheelchair and immediately asked about Carl. He was compelled to tell them Carl was now missing but everyone was working diligently to find him and Lt. Brigida. She turned her back on them and returned to her room in an agitated state.

Chad was intent on calming Jeri. He repeated what Carl had told him how he had been trapped to work for Hadi. It was to save their lives.

Jeri mumbled, "I don't know what to believe anymore."

By now the ambassador had joined them and chimed in, saying he had just submitted his resignation by wire to President Garrett and asked that they all be brought home at once. According to Robbins, he also told the president that Gamba was too dangerous and that they hate all Americans. They wanted no part of it. He finished by asking Chad to bring Carl home, "but only if you firmly believe in him."

"I'm still very confused with his actions despite what you told me. He had plenty of opportunities to right the situation but chose not to. Then take his relationship with my daughter—I was told he had not slept with her for some time. Add to that the servant's gossip that he had someone else."

Washington called a couple of hours later, advising the ambassador that were sending a special forces commando team headed by Captain Spud Turner. The objective was to sneak into Karner and bring the hostages back alive. Intelligence was pinning the location down to a city called Sorcha and a specific hiding place. The Karner government had excused the kidnappings as an act of a terrorist group. Washington had no choice but to depend on a rescue by the commando team. Chad was appointed as liaison and permitted to participate in the rescue effort.

When Spud arrived, he questioned Chad at length. Chad had painted Carl as a victim, but the captain wasn't buying that version. He continually shook his head during the interview. Chad sized him up as a six foot four headstrong Ranger who believed in straight talk and action, not words. Now with some doubts, Chad started to feel the pangs of guilt for Nellie's life because of his misguided sympathy for Carl.

The plan was simple but foolproof. Two vehicles would cross the border at night. The attack would take place at midnight. The two-story wooden house had been located at Nineteen Zagard Street. It had two entrances, front and back. Spud detailed that four would crash the rear and front. Tear gas would be used to disable and minimize the expected defense by Hadi and his men. Unfortunately, it was unknown as to the number of terrorists in the building and the nature of their fire power. According to Spud, "The whole thing is a crapshoot."

The trip to the border was uneventful, but the full moon gave so much light, they were fearful of being seen. Spud found a way one mile from the checkpoint that would bring them to a road leading into the city. From the border to the house was a distance of twenty-eight miles. As they entered Sorcha, the streets were empty and dimly lit.

Locating the destination was easily accomplished. Voices could be heard from the interior as the commandoes took their position. There was one guard, and Tex, a super Ranger, was dispersed to take him out. Once that was done, Spud warned Chad not to do anything foolish that would place Carl and Nellie in harm's way. He then gave the order to move in. There was gunfire from the rear of the first floor. Someone released the tear gas, making it difficult to appraise the area, but Spud found a door to the basement and they went full force down the steps. There was a guard at the bottom with a machine gun. Before he could do anything, a commando took him out.

In the basement, they were confronted by Hadi holding a gun to Nellie's head and Carl lying prone on the floor as if he was dead. Nellie looked bad and disoriented. Her face and head were bloodied and bruised. Her clothes had been ripped to shreds with only her black bra and panties showing. She had a gag in her mouth that prevented her from screaming.

Hadi yelled in a heavy Middle Eastern accent, "I will allow her to live if you allow me to leave to continue my fight against your country, in the name of Allah."

Spud responded, "Give it up. The whole building is surrounded. You'll never make it out of here alive."

Suddenly and most unexpectedly, Carl rolled over and grabbed Hadi's leg. He reacted by turning to Carl and shooting him in the chest.

Nellie dove out of the way, and Spud fired a shot into Hadi's head. Carl's action made it possible to kill Hadi and rid the world of his terrorism.

They immediately ran over to Nellie and removed the gag.

She said, "I'm all right. Go help Carl."

Chad went over, but it was too late. Carl was dead.

CHAPTER 17

The team transported Nellie and Carl's body back to the border. From there she was airlifted along with Chad to Wiesbaden, Germany.

Captain Wilkes met them at the hospital for a debriefing. Nellie was unable to speak but was able to write about how Hadi had tortured Carl and her. She also wrote that Hadi had shot Carl moments before the team appeared in the basement.

Chad and the captain were at her bedside for three days. During that time she did not speak. The doctor said it was all psychological and it was possible that she might never speak again. He said they would be shipping her to a special hospital in the states.

On the flight home Captain Wilkes told Chad that he had very bad news. Maria's mutilated body was found in a dumpster outside an apartment complex in Baltimore. She had been strangled to death. There had been no clues as to her killer.

Chad was taken aback and asked Wilkes why he didn't give the news beforehand. The captain answered that Chad had too much on his plate and he thought it wasn't the proper time to tell him of Maria's death.

Chad immediately reacted by blaming himself. He was intent on finding the person or persons responsible for Maria's murder. He could not refrain from concluding that the real target was himself. They kept killing people around him, and that had to stop.

He asked Captain Wilkes for permission to try to solve these murders after he handled Carl's funeral. There was no hesitation to approve Chad's request.

Carl's body was shipped to Dover Air Base, Delaware. The family made burial arrangements, but Chad's intervention allowed him to be interred in Arlington.

The day of the funeral was a dark and gloomy one. The Robbins family was terribly distraught, feeling very guilty about their mixed emotions concerning Carl. Jeri was quite stoic, apparently under a heavy tranquillizer. Koski and his whole family were there. They were Carl's only living relatives and were carrying on at the gravesite.

Chad was the target of their stares and evil looks. Ten feet to the left was a tall man in his mid-thirties who appeared very familiar to him. Chad was able to place him as the man who was in the black Lincoln following him and Maria. He turned to the left and saw the black Lincoln parked with the other cars. His instincts told him this was Mr. Zero, the arsonist, office bomber, drug dealer, and murderer, all wrapped into one. This had to be his starting point.

The congressman took Chad aside and said, "That's my son, Gustav."

Chad answered, "I think I've seen him around. Listen, I tried to cover for Carl, but he was in too deep. However he certainly deserve a hero's burial for his last effort to make things right."

Koski responded facetiously, "He was lucky to have you as a roommate and a friend. I guess you want us to believe you had nothing to do with him getting killed."

As Chad walked away, he said, "I don't know what you mean, but in spite of himself, I was trying to save him."

Gustav approached Chad and threatened, "From now on, you're going to be seeing a lot more of me—see you around." He then turned and marched away, casting mean looks at Jeri and Chad.

He was left with a sick feeling in the pit of his stomach and realized that this was a forewarning of things to come. Chad then turned his attention to the Robbins family and went over to where they were standing.

Oddly, Mrs. Robbins was standing by herself, a distance away from the others. She was sobbing heavily and that appeared to be very strange to Chad.

The Honor Guard did the customary service but were not permitted to play taps. The congressman gave a eulogy in his mother tongue and then walked away. They stayed until the coffin was lowered into the ground.

All Chad could visualize were the touchdown passes and Carl dancing under the goal posts. It really didn't say too much about their relationship.

He then went over to Ginny Robbins to express his condolences but she turned away.

He asked the ambassador, "What do you make of that?"

The response was, "She loved him like a son and will not forgive us. It will be a long time before she comes around, but you and I have much to discuss. Please call me soon."

Now Chad was totally confused, so he uttered a weak good-bye. As he left the cemetery, he remembered that it was February 19, his birthday.

CHAPTER 18

Meanwhile, Nellie had been evacuated to the naval hospital at Bethesda, Maryland. Chad would visit each day but became rather discouraged with her progress. She still could not speak, and it seemed that her mind was beginning to wander beyond reality. He would bring a pad and write messages to her.

At the outset Nellie would answer but in time that stopped. Furthermore, her eyes were closed most of the time. When they were opened it was like she was in a zombie-like trance.

Dr. Soble thought she was regressing and advised treatment at a long-term facility. He told Chad that the torture had ravaged her and had taken a toll on her mind. His final prediction was that maybe in time with a series of shock treatments, Nellie could be restored to what she was.

A week later Nellie was shipped to a government facility in Poughkeepsie, New York. Chad was asked to ride with her in the ambulance. It was a long and boring ride. He could not wait until they arrived at the hospital.

She was taken to a private room and administered to by a head nurse who resembled Nurse Ratched from the movie *One Flew over the Cuckoo's Nest*. She was sullen, hard-looking, and very curt. He was asked to leave while they prepared her for her stay. When he went back to the room, Nellie was already sleeping as a result of medication given to her.

Nurse Ratched said to him, "Don't come here too much, it's not too good for her."

Not knowing what she meant, Chad began to argue but thought better and walked away cursing to himself.

His assignment was to remain in Washington and train new recruits to the program. After a while, curiosity got the better of him, and he called the ambassador. They exchanged several calls before connecting and finally arranged to meet at the Washington Hilton. The meeting took place about three months after Carl's burial. Mr. Robbins immediately told him that his wife was holding them both responsible for Carl's death and was saying they put him in harm's way.

"By the way, Jeri wants to visit with you for old times' sake. My boy, I think she wants to make up for lost time."

His body sparked with sexual thoughts of her and suddenly a loss of memory for Nellie. "When can I see her?"

"She's in town now, so maybe you can have dinner tonight around eight o' clock.:

When Chad entered the Lobby, he spotted Jeri by the bar dressed in a very tight black pant suit that magnified her sexy body. As he approached her, he noticed that she was nervous and her cheeks were flushed. Chad sensed she'd had a couple of drinks in anticipation of their meeting.

He kissed her on the cheek and suggested they go to Giovanni's, a small Italian restaurant on New York Avenue. While they were waiting for their food, Jeri opened up and held the floor for the next forty-five minutes.

"When I was dating him, I thought I loved him. After our marriage, he became a totally different person. Carl became rude and abusive to me. He hated and disrespected my father but seemed to really get along with my mother. It was then that I realized that I didn't love him and was stuck in this bad relationship. Many times I asked why he'd changed, but he would give me the silent treatment. In a very weak moment on my part, we had sex and I got pregnant. That appeared to make him a lot happier, and I was counting on the baby turning things around for us. But when I lost the baby, things went downhill pretty fast."

They stopped to eat their food and then she continued without a pause. "Upon our assignment to the embassy, he became even worse. Carl's attitude was awful. It wasn't long after that he took up with Hadi. They would have these long conversations that appeared that Hadi was ordering him about. Further strange was the fact that my husband would have spirited conversations with my mother and would not talk to me for days. She always had a special relationship with Carl. From the outset, she doted on him as if he was her only child. Mom actually tossed me aside for him.

"He never spoke to my dad other than business or when other dignitaries were present. We had stopped sleeping together before we went to Gamba. That was when I realized that I really missed you but could not reach out for you. Carl and Hadi took over the daily routine of the embassy and then the business of the ambassador. They would inspect the mail my father received and did everything to erode his powers. My mother and I were pretty much confined to our rooms. For some reason she had more liberty than me. I attributed that to her serious MS condition.

"Dad spent most of his time in his office, doing very little. I didn't complain because I feared for our lives. My father would complain to me but refused to notify Washington because he was intimidated and embarrassed."

Jeri took a long sip of wine and said, "I need a break."

They finished their meal and went back to the hotel. At the bar area, she began. "What I am going to tell you is the strangest part. One of the maids left an envelope in my room that was intended for my mother. I was nosy and opened it with care. Inside was a smaller envelope with writing on the outside that said, "Ginny, this is important. Please give it to Carl. Love always, George.

"The message was in a Slovak language. I had always felt that my mom was sharing secrets with Carl, and now my instincts had been verified.

"I immediately put the two envelopes together and asked the maid to leave it in my mother's room. Frankly, I didn't know what to make of it and discussed it with my father. It was then that he told me that they had not slept together for some time. That wasn't news to me as I had surmised that on my own. But what really bothered my father was that she was so distant and cold to us both. The envelope was our very first clue that Mom had a relationship with George Koski, Carl's uncle. I had always suspected him to be my mother's lover.

"After that discovery, I continued to look for other signs, without success. Mom and Carl continued their private conversations. When I confronted Carl about these conversations, he would say that that they were discussing her condition. I then asked him what was going on in the embassy, and he answered, 'Don't ask too many questions.' Carl then told me he was functioning under tremendous pressure and was concerned for all our lives. I told him outright that I didn't believe him."

CHAPTER 19

The next night Chad met Jeri in her suite at the hotel. They didn't waste any time. He took her into his arms and kissed her. She kissed him back with plenty of passion. They discarded their clothes and ran to each other. Once again he saw those beautiful breasts, reminiscent of his childhood experience.

Jeri then whispered to him, "Please make love to me. All these years I wanted only you but somehow it never worked out."

He placed her on the bed. During the act, he thought, *This is the one I always wanted, and now that I finally have her, I will not lose her.*

That night was glorious, and so were the many others that followed—filled with much passion. By then they realized how much they wanted each other and began to talk about marriage.

The Robbins family had returned to the family home in Quenton, and fortuitously, Chad had been assigned to Ocean Academy as an intelligence strategy adjunct professor. The house was about twenty minutes from the school, and he went there every night to be with her. Jeri was a great cook, so they ate in most nights. There were only three at the dinner table. Ginny, who had severe MS, took her meals in her second-floor apartment. She had daytime help, and Jeri would cover until she went to sleep.

The ambassador was very friendly to Chad, but one could see that the Gamba experience had affected his mental processes. He would ramble on every subject, making it impossible to carry on a sensible conversation.

Chad would listen and from time to time even say something. Nine o'clock was their quiet time. If they wanted to make love, they went to

Jeri's room and then Chad would stay over until morning. Keeping some of his clothes at her house made it easy for him.

It was a comfortable arrangement, except that Mrs. Robbins would have nothing to do with him. In her mind, Chad was the cause of Carl being killed, and that was that. He couldn't fathom why Ginny hated him so much, especially since when he was a teenager she'd loved him like a son.

Naval intelligence was investigating Gustav Koski to determine his involvement with the admiral's house fire and the London bombing. The results were negative and were further bolstered by his record of no past criminal activity. Presently, he was listed as a legislative aide to his father and owner of a very Yuppie bar in DC. Ernie Jinks was a silent partner. He had served his time and had resumed life in the fast lane.

They were an odd couple. Gustav was tall and wiry while Ernie had more of a fireplug physique.

Intelligence decided to maintain a soft surveillance on both. Kit had been released, and his present whereabouts were unknown. That bothered Chad, because Kit was a very dangerous man.

He told Jeri about Nellie and how guilty he felt about being so happy while she was wasting away in a hospital. She was very understanding and suggested they both visit her. Chad understood this as her attempt to make him feel better but also put an end to that lingering relationship he had with Nellie. A couple of days later they drove to see her by route of the New Jersey Turnpike and the New York Thruway. The scenery of picturesque fall leaves and the great weather helped eased the anxiety of the trip.

Upon arrival, they were directed to an outer garden, where Nellie was seated in a chair with a large blanket around her. Her hair was undone, and she had lost a lot of weight. She was all skin and bones. Nellie would not raise her head or respond to them.

The visit was futile. Chad tried to tell her that she could be helped, but it was apparent that she had drifted to another world. Nellie could never be part of his life again.

The next few months were pretty uneventful. They consisted of the same routine that a married couple would experience. With that thought in mind, Chad surprised Jeri with a three carat diamond ring and proposed that they get married by Father Pat as soon as possible. Jeri wanted a simple wedding with a small reception.

Two days after the proposal, Chad was walking up the long and windy driveway to her house, when he heard a clamor, a door slam, and people running in an opposite direction. It was broad daylight but he didn't see anyone.

His attention was drawn to the library area where moaning signs were originating.

The ambassador was lying dead in the doorway in a pool of blood. Chad turned his attention to Jeri. She had been stabbed repeatedly and was barely alive. Chad took her into his arms, pleading with Jeri to hold on.

She murmured with her last breath, "It was them."

The jagged knife was lying next to her body and out of instinct, he picked it up. He kept yelling, "Why, why?"

A few minutes later the police arrived. He assumed Mrs. Robbins had called them.

She was covered with blood, and he was holding the knife. Chad was incoherent, out of control, and likely a suspect.

He was brought to police headquarters and placed in an interrogation room. Two detectives entered the room and questioned him over an eight-hour period. He kept telling them that he had seen Mrs. Robbins at the top of the stairs but she had disappeared. This went on and on until Father Pat showed up. He was the police chaplain, and as a courtesy, the prosecutor allowed Father Pat to take him to the rectory.

Two days later they arrested him at Jeri's wake at Cascella's Funeral Home. The charge was murder in the first degree, with the death sentence looming over his head. He never got the chance to go to her burial as he was being held without bail.

CHAPTER 20

CHAPTER 20

Subsequent to his arrest and indictment, Chad was relieved of his duties at the academy. He was reassigned to a local recruiting office in Baltimore. The move was made to afford him the extra time to prepare his defense.

His first act was to get legal representation, so he sought out Judd Baker, a young and distinguished criminal attorney. He had met him at a military trial where Judd had represented a young sailor who had been accused of a series of robberies aboard his ship. The sailor was acquitted because of his skill of cross-examination and creative thinking. Chad admired Judd's bulldog approach and thought that would be needed in his defense.

The venue of the trial was set at the Quenton Superior Court where the ruling judge was the Honorable Mary Bryant.

Chad asked Judd to get the trial out of that court because of the judge. She was a political appointee from the Democratic Party and was known to have a strong dislike for Chad Sr. Her husband, Matthew, had been his opponent for mayor in three elections. Each time Chad Sr. had mounted personal campaigns against him.

The history was that Matthew, while president of the Board of Education, sponsored a bond issue to construct a new high school. Under his watch, the cost overran, amounting to five million dollars. The investigation that followed disclosed that the female superintendent of schools was romantically linked to the general contractor. The media continually criticized Bryant for his lack of oversight, and Chad Sr. used it as ammunition in the campaigns. Matthew Bryant passed away from lung cancer after the last contested election. Judge Mary Bryant never forgave Chad Sr.

Judd made a motion for a change of venue because of overall prejudice toward Chad resulting from publicity and a failure to have a fair trial in that jurisdiction.

She immediately denied the application without comment. He then requested that the judge recuse herself in view of the history of the two families. She denied that motion based on the ruling that the court is and would be objective in the approaching trial. It was predicted that it would be a four to six week trial. The state announced that they would present three witnesses, the coroner, chief detective Manny Rose, and Ginny Robbins. Chad was shocked that she would be testifying for the state because of all people, she knew he didn't do it.

Manny Rose was another story. He was definitely not friendly to Chad. It all surfaced when they were teammates on the high school football team. Chad gave him a dressing down in the locker room because he missed key blocks, and Chad was sacked several times, resulting in a concussion. Manny was to blame but did not enjoy the embarrassment heaped upon him.

From that moment on he had nothing but contempt for Chad. Judd asked Chad as to what he told Manny at headquarters. He answered nothing. That did not stop Manny for holding him for eight hours with continuous questioning.

Before opening statements, Judd renewed his motion to have the judge recuse herself. She denied the motion and said to Chad, "Wipe that sarcastic smile from your face. You're going to toe the line in this courtroom—and that goes for you, Mr. Baker."

From that moment on she was a second prosecutor at the trial. During the jury selection, Judge Bryant made it clear that there would be sequestration of the jury for at least four weeks, if not longer. They were told to bring clothes for that period and that they would be housed at the Windsor Motel. That immediately built a wall of hate against Chad as they would be apart from their families for that period.

By Maryland law, each side was allowed eight peremptory challenges in jury selections. In addition, counsel could ask the court to dismiss a potential juror for established cause. It was up to the judge to rule on the substance of that request. The object of using a "cause" challenge was to save a free challenge that could be used without explanation.

The most noteworthy was the case of juror Jessie Wicks. Judd had asked that she be excused because she had been Mitzi's secretary-receptionist for three years. On voir dire, a preliminary examination of a witness or juror by a judge or counsel, Judd had established that she had been fired from the job, but Jessie insisted she could be fair. Judd didn't believe her and argued to the court that this was a classic example of how the actions of the mother may subconsciously affect the ultimate decision of this juror. The judge denied the motion, and Judd was forced to use his last challenge.

The last juror needed to fill the box was to be selected, and Judd had no challenge to exercise. That juror was Johnny Blaine, a former maverick councilman who had served with Chad Sr. He was a union delegate for the carpenters and won elections because he was able to turn out the blue collar workers of Quenton. Johnny would make an abundance of promises to lower taxes, but he never delivered. He was a loud and disturbing factor in the governing body.

Chad made it known that Johnny and his father never got along. Also, he had hit on his mother, and she had embarrassed him in public.

The judge refused to excuse him for cause and rebuked Baker, saying, "It's not my fault that you used your challenges unwisely and have no more."

Thus the jury was selected and comprised of eight women and four men. To cap her dislike for Chad, she named Johnny Blaine as foreman.

She ruled against Chad on every evidentiary motion made by Judd. She went out of her way to demean Judd and paint him as incompetent in the eyes of the jury.

Prosecutor Tom Jergens said in his opening statement, "Chad Braden had a strong motive to kill his future father-in-law. Mrs. Robbins will testify that two days before the murders she had given him a note explaining that her husband was the cause of his parents' deaths."

Judd jumped up and asked for a sidebar, where he asked the judge to exclude the note and related testimony because the note was found in Chad's clothing while he was in police headquarters before any arrest occurred. It was a product of an unlawful search.

Judge Bryant turned to Jergens and said, "What you have to say to that?"

He answered, "Detective Rose will confirm that Chad gave him the note voluntarily."

Baker argued that it could have never happened that way, and the judge said, "You'll have your chance at Rose on cross-examination. Meanwhile, go on, Mr. Jergens."

They returned to their tables.

Jergens continued his opening statement. "The note explained that Jamie and Mrs. Braden were caught in an illicit love affair, and once Chad Sr. found out, he killed himself and his wife. For about fifteen years Chad and his brother, Pat, were unaware of what caused their father to commit the murder-suicide. When Chad found out, he decided to kill Jamie, but his fiancée got in his way. He killed her as well. Mrs. Robbins will testify how she observed Chad committing the brutal murders."

Upon hearing that, Chad knew he was sunk. Mrs. Robbins was a sympathetic witness, and the jury would no doubt believe her. For the life of him he could not understand why Ginny hated him so much.

When he was a youngster, she used to kiss him and run her hands through his wavy hair. She would then say," Go get 'em, tiger!"

Manny Rose was the first witness for the prosecution and provided damaging testimony about how the police found Chad holding the knife over Jeri's body, blood all over his clothing and prints all over the house. He testified how Chad was incoherent at the scene but regained his composure at headquarters. During questioning and after he had refused a lawyer, he took the note from his pants and gave it to the detectives. They asked him why he was carrying it around on his person and he had no answer.

When Judd crossed him, he asked, "Isn't a fact that Chad told you that he wanted to show his brother, Pat, the note and then together confront Jamie?"

Manny said, "I never heard that."

The next witness was the coroner, Dr. Jamison. His role was limited to the identification of the bodies and description of the wounds and fatal blows. The prosecutor showed him a series of twenty pictures and asked for a verbal description that satisfied the court. His testimony took about three hours and in all was rather boring. The jurors were nodding and were very restless during his testimony.

The state wasted no time producing Ginny Robbins. Once she had been a strikingly beautiful lady, and now she was an invalid, prisoner of a wheelchair. Her whole looks and appearance had changed. She no longer was the well-dressed neat freak but just a plain old lady.

Ginny told the jury, "I cannot walk because of MS so I always sit in my chair in my apartment. My husband had an elevator installed for me, but I rarely went downstairs. On the day of the murders, I heard noises and came out of my room to see what was happening. It was then I saw Chad holding this big knife and standing over my daughter's body. I immediately turned around, went into my room, locked the door, and called the police." She then pointed at Chad and said, "That's him. He's the killer."

Chad then yelled, "Ginny, why are you doing this to me? It wasn't me! I loved your daughter."

Judge Bryant ordered the bailiff to remove him from the courtroom to a room where the proceedings could be transmitted to him. After instructing the jury to disregard the comments from Chad, she turned to attorney Baker and said she would allow him back in the morning.

The next morning the judge threatened to remove him permanently other than when he would testify. Chad told her, "Do whatever you want with me. I don't expect anything that is even close to being fair from you." She backed off during the rest of the trial.

Baker tried to cross-examine Ginny as to what exactly she had observed, implying that she hadn't seen Chad commit the murders. But she was unrelenting. "It *was* Chad," she insisted, "because I saw him holding the knife and stabbing my daughter's body. There was no one else in the house!" With that she'd made her case. There wasn't too much more Baker could do with her, so he told the court he was finished with Mrs. Robbins. The state then rested their case.

Now it was time for the defense. The first part of the defense was to parade a slew of character witnesses who exclaimed that Chad could never done the killings as it was against his DNA. Chad then testified. He made an excellent witness. The prosecutor failed to budge him as he detailed how he found the ambassador and Jeri.

But despite his testimony, it seemed to no avail as it appeared that this jury seemed ready to convict him. All throughout Ginny's testimony, they were smiling and looking directly at her. When Chad testified, they were looking away from him.

When asked about the note, he told them how he got the note from Mrs. Robbins two days before the tragedies. He offered how he was going to confront the ambassador for an explanation, not kill him. He realized his own mother had a lot to do with the illicit affair.

During his direct, he was also asked if he had seen Mrs. Robbins that day. He responded that he did and she was at the top of the stairs and then disappeared into her room. It wasn't much after that when the police arrived.

Judd gave a stirring closing statement and kept driving home that there was a mountain of circumstantial evidence that presented an overwhelming area of reasonable doubt. His main point was they no one saw Chad commit the murders.

Unfortunately, the jury only took four hours to convict him, and Judge Bryant immediately sentenced him to death. She cited that the murders were heinous crimes and that Chad deserved to die as the jury has spoken.

They took Chad away in handcuffs.

Afterward, two jurors approached attorney Baker and told him how Johnny Blaine was obsessed in finding Chad guilty. The jurors confessed how they blindly followed him and were astonished how he kept on repeating that the judge knew he was guilty. He also speculated that the judge was going to sentence him to death. It was like he knew for certain.

Judd later met with Chad and advised him that the bias of the court and prejudicial behavior of Johnny Blaine were great grounds of appeal. Chad didn't have much hope in that expression of optimism.

CHAPTER 21

CHAPTER 21

C had was shipped the next day to the Bronson State Prison located in Germantown, Maryland. It was an old facility housing about four hundred inmates. Upon arriving there, he was the object of many evil stares and vulgar obscenities. That upset him to no end because he was fearful of what was going to be next. Fortunately, two days later he met Chuck, a bald African American who was the main trustee. Chuck said for $10,000 he would provide Chad with advice and the influence of his position. Translated, that meant he would be Chad's protector. He accepted and arranged to have the money delivered to Chuck's sister in Baltimore.

Chad had been there for about five months without incident when Judd wrote him and stated that the appeal had been denied. The only remaining procedure was to have the governor pardon him or save him from the gas chamber. Meanwhile he would be shipped to death row at the XOR Prison in Taneytown within a week.

A day later he was standing in the chow line when a Slavic man confronted and pushed him. This man was part of a clique of prisoners who were of the same ethnic background. They were about ten men strong and threw their weight around, intimidating the population.

Chad gently slipped away and sat next to Chuck. Chuck said, "I saw what happened there. You'd better watch yourself 'cause you're definitely a target, and I can't protect you every minute."

Later that day Chad was standing in the outside triangle getting his one hour of fresh air when this same Slavic man again came toward him. Chad glanced at his hand and saw that he was holding a shiv. Chad, utilizing his combat training, disarmed and wrestled him to the ground. Onlookers immediately dispersed when the guards arrived.

They had observed his actions and slated him for solitary confinement.

Nothing happened to this other man as there was no shiv in sight to see. Chad speculated that someone had picked it up and hid it.

It was a boon for him to be in solitary confinement as it prevented further attacks. Chad was released from solitary the day before he was to report to XOR Prison's death row. Chad said to Chuck that he needed to get the Slavic man who jumped him, Iggy, and find out what was going on.

Chuck said, "You're crazy. How do you expect to get him alone?" Then he thought a little more and said to Chad," This fellow Iggy usually takes a shower in the right wing at night. Maybe that's your best bet."

Luckily, Chad's cell was in the right wing.

That night he followed Iggy into the shower room. No one else was there. He pinned him against the wall and asked about who was directing Iggy to kill him. Iggy responded by saying, "Let me go."

Chad asked again, and Iggy gave the same answer. That prompted Chad to say, "Fuck you," and in one swift move broke his neck. He slipped back to his cell without anyone seeing him.

Four hours later the guards came to his cell. Chad feared that he had been discovered and they were arresting him. Instead, they said, "Get up. We're taking you to XOR."

The ride was about two hours away. He knew exactly where it was because he had visited someone in XOR during an investigation. The new hi-tech facility was nestled in the picturesque surrounding woods. He remembered that during his visit, two inmates occupied one cell, but there was an alarm in each cell that could be activated by the inmate who was being attacked.

He was taken to death row. The cell was four by five and reeked of urine. Chad had thought the accommodations would be better. He was there for an hour when he realized he was the only inmate.

Butch the guard interrupted his daydreaming by yelling, "Tell me, killer, how do you expect to spend your last days in our hotel?"

Chad knew it wasn't going to be easy from herein.

Chad began to have severe headaches and recurring nightmares. They were always the same. The predominant figure was a tall woman dressed in black with a hood. However, he could never make out the face. She would always scream at Chad, "I'll get you eventually, but in the meantime I will get your loved ones."

During his waking hours he visualized the death mask and smelled the gas as his life ebbed away. The date of the execution was set for sixty-two days away, and Chad was having a hard time dealing with the prospect of dying. Thus he turned to God and began to pray nonstop.

Luckily, his brother, Pat, had gone to the seminary with Warden Conlin's brother so he allowed Pat to visit often. The warden graciously offered his office for their visits.

As time went by, Chad became concerned about his brother's health. He had this hacking cough that probably originated as a result of heavy smoking during his early years. Pat was his only conduit to the outside world. The visits were very spiritual and filled with lots of prayer.

Chad remained depressed about his future, but Pat was optimistic that the Lord would save him.

Every morning at about six, Tony Long, the inmate paralegal, would visit and discuss Chad's legal problem. Tony was the typical jailhouse lawyer who completed a certification program that allowed him to interact with death row prisoners. At the time Tony was serving a life sentence for brutally murdering his stepfather and had already served twenty years.

For the last several days he had been preaching to Chad about getting rid of Judd Baker as his attorney. His point was that Judd's strategy had been wrong in attacking Judge Bryant. He preached that Chad should get "Irish Jim" Brady to approach the governor for consideration of a life sentence, therefore giving Chad more time to find the real killer.

Tony said, "Your only chance is to get Irish Jim to represent you. So far your appeals have gotten you nowhere. Let me tell you what he did for me. I was forty-two years old and living with my mother and stepfather. The only reason I was there was because I didn't want to leave my mother alone with that bastard. I had a drinking problem, but it was nothing compared to his evil attitude. He was forever yelling, cursing, and threatening my mother. Hate began to build up in me until I couldn't stop it. One day, he punched her in the face, making her bleed from the nose like a faucet. I went berserk, jumped him, tied him to a chair, and tortured him until he died. It was a gruesome scene, and when the police arrived, I surrendered.

They gave me a public defender who used an insanity defense that didn't work.

"I was found guilty because the prosecutor successfully argued that I knew what I was doing and therefore the killing was premeditated. The judge sentenced me to death. Irish Jim decided to take my case on a pro bono basis.

"He went back to the Supreme Court, but they refused to take action. Next he went to the governor, who eventually gave me clemency and a reduction to life. I cheated death and maybe you can too."

Once Tony left, Chad was determined to reach out to Irish Jim Brady.

Chad fell asleep and was awakened by Butch hitting the bars with his night stick. "Hey, killer, they want you up in the warden's office."

It was only eight in the morning. Pat usually came about eleven. Chad wondered if something had happened.

When he arrived at the office, there were two state investigators who said they were interested in the killing at the Bronson prison. The blonde detective, Darla Wilson, was intent on implicating Chad. She asked if wanted an attorney present, and he said no.

The other investigator, Detective Jerry Suarez, appeared younger and kept following his partner's lead. He said to Chad, "Let me get right to the point. Do you know the main trustee, Chuck? Well, he's fighting for his life right now because a group of Slavs beat him to a pulp in retaliation for the death of their friend Iggy. You knew Iggy, right?"

"Yeah, I had a couple of run-ins with him that landed me in solitary. After I got out, I never saw him again. I was transferred here, and that's all there is."

Detective Wilson added, "We think you know more, so stop playing games."

"Detectives, come and see me anytime, but make sure it's before I'm executed. By my last count, that's in forty days."

After they left, Warden Colin suggested Chad wait in his office for Pat.

When Pat came in he hugged his younger brother hard with emotion. He looked sad. This scared Chad because he had never seen Pat this way and thought perhaps he was throwing in the towel.

Chad said, "You have to get Irish Jim Brady to represent me and try to do something. Use the rest of my trust money, but do it now."

Pat's eyes lit up with hope, and he said, "I know him from the cathedral. He always came to have dinner with Cardinal Burke. They went to St. Justin's Grammar School together. You're probably right, he'll help you. I'll try to get him here as soon as possible."

Pat's mood immediately lightened, and now he was smiling and laughing. They talked for an hour, entertaining themselves with stories from their childhood.

Chad said, "Remember when Dad caught us looking at Cynthia next door through the binoculars? She was totally naked, and even you were salivating. You threw the binoculars out the window hoping Dad wouldn't catch on. Boy, was he ever so mad."

"What about the time that Mom and Dad went away and we slept over at the Robbins's place? We were treated like kings by Ginny and Jeri. I still picture her coming to breakfast in her PJs. Her nipples were shining through like lanterns. Right then I wanted to run away with her. How can they say I killed Jeri when I loved her so much?"

Pat said, "Have faith it will work out."

Chad responded, "It's easy for you to say, but the bottom line is the execution is coming up fast."

Now Chad had something else to be concerned about.

CHAPTER 22

Irish Jim visited the next day, and for the first time, Chad experienced a faint ray of hope. Jim asked Chad to tell him everything.

Chad responded, "I don't know what happened at Jeri's house that day. Walking toward the door, I thought I heard a scream and footsteps of people running. I opened the front door with my key and immediately heard moaning coming from the library. As I advanced, I saw Mr. Robbins lying in the doorway. He appeared to be dead. Jeri was near him and was barely alive. She had been stabbed repeatedly and was bleeding profusely. I took her into my arms. As she took her last breath, she said, 'It was them.' The knife was lying next to her body and I picked it up. Someone called the police.

"When the police arrived I was incoherent and out of control. There was blood all over my clothes from my holding her. They then interrogated me for six hours at police headquarters."

Since he had not read the transcript, Jim asked Chad to tell him everything. Irish Jim asked, "What did you tell them? Did they ask you about the note that came up in your trial?"

"I told them I was going to confront the ambassador to hear his side. I completely understood that my mother had something to do with the affair."

"Did you see Mrs. Robbins at all when you were in the house?"

"Yes, I saw her at the top of the stairway. I called out to her but she disappeared. Within minutes the police were there."

Jim then said to Chad, "The warden gave me permission to give you this tape recorder. I want you to record everything about your past associations within the last fifteen years, from your high school days to that fateful day, as well as any other thoughts you may have about your predicament. Do this soon because it may help me build a case for you. By the way, your brother Pat got a visit from Annie Brown. She's your friend Chuck's sister and works in the Bronson Prison front office. It seems that Chuck will survive his injuries and will be released when they determine he is okay.

"Meanwhile, she is asking for help for him when he is released. He needs a place to stay and maybe do some light work. She also said for you to be careful because they are out to get you."

"What does that mean, Mr. Brady?"

"Call me Irish."

"Irish, I owe this guy big time. He took a bad beating because he befriended me while I was at Bronson. Tell Pat to take him in and give him a driver's job. If he needs money, tell Pat to take it from the trust. There's more than enough in there. As far as this other problem is concerned, I did have a fight with this guy called Iggy. Somebody killed him, but it wasn't me. There are these two investigators trying to implicate me in his murder. I told them I knew nothing about Iggy's death and that night I was being transferred to XOR. But I think she means that his countrymen are looking out to kill me."

"Okay, my friend. Butch will look out for you. I'll give him some green and he will take care of the relief man as well."

"I'm glad you know him because he has been a major pain in the ass since I got here."

"Chad, believe me, the man owes me big time. He'll take care of you."

"Irish, what are you going to do next?"

"I'm going to find Ginny Robbins and talk to her."

"Good luck, because that woman hates me."

"Maybe I can get her to change her mind and get to the truth. I have to go. Stay strong. I'll see you in a couple of days. Remember, only talk to me and your brother, not even Tony Long."

It was nine thirty in the morning. Chad had been dozing when he heard the relief guard, John Neary, moaning. He looked up and saw a man dressed in a green workman's uniform trying to open the lock to his cell. Fortunately, there was a double lock and he was having a hard time getting in.

He was a young man and said to Chad in a very heavy Slavic accent, "I'm here to avenge my father's death." Just then a shot rang out and the intruder fell to the floor.

The blood was splattered all over the floor as he had been shot in the head by another guard, Jake. Jake had been sneaking down the corridor unnoticed by the young man. Jake grew suspicious when he realized he was not an employee of Slaton Plumbing and Heating.

After he admitted him, another guard said to Jake, "They were here last week when you were out and they only come every three months for inspections."

According to Jake, he grabbed a weapon and took the shot when he saw John on the floor. John had been stabbed in the neck with a screwdriver and was bleeding profusely.

Chad thought that this had all the makings of a plot to kill him, and possibly someone from the jail was in on it.

John Neary was fighting for his life, and the media converged on the warden for a statement.

It was apparent that Chad's death sentence would be used as the vehicle for a media circus. It was implied that the intruder was not there to kill Chad but to break him out. When the warden and the investigators tried to question him, he referred them to Irish Jim. Chad was being vilified and could not give a sufficient explanation as to what took place.

Pat and Irish came to see him five hours later and were only permitted to speak to him via telephone. They had heard the news and were concerned with his safety.

Jim said, "Play it cool. You don't know this man or what he was up to. You perceived yourself as the next victim once he got the cell lock open. That's it and nothing else. It's ridiculous to think it was a breakout. What was the remainder of that plan? Meanwhile, maybe Neary can shed some light—if he survives."

Chad said, "I don't think I'm safe here. They must have someone from the inside helping them. At this rate it's a race to who gets me first, the Russians or the state. But the bottom line is that I am convinced that don't treat the situation as if I am a target but seem to adhere to the escape scenario concocted by the press. Are they going to protect me or not?"

Jim said, "Let me give you some good news. My investigator located Mrs. Robbins. Her cousin Matilda Blaine said she is in a nursing home in Ashville, North Carolina."

"Did you say Matilda Blaine? Johnny Blaine's wife?"

"No, she's his sister."

"So Johnny Blaine, my foreman, was a cousin to the main witness against me."

Jim answered, "Chad, consider it good news. This may be the break that you need and makes it more important that we speak to Mrs. Robbins and Johnny Blaine. If they framed you, we need to know why and how."

Chad then said rather sarcastically, "Good luck. I don't hold out too much hope for her. As for Johnny, I don't know."

CHAPTER 23

The next morning Jim was at the jail with news about Neary. He surprised Chad by telling him that Neary recovered and backed Chad because just before he lost consciousness he heard the attacker say he was there to avenge his father's death. Jim said the breakout theory was history and then explained that Annie Brown call Pat and told him Chuck had died.

"She said she had seen on TV about the attempt on your life and wanted to see me.

"Yesterday she was at my office and said she was very sorry for your troubles. She said Chuck had told her that you wanted to confront Iggy and that their conversation took place in the jail and was overheard by another guard. It was her assumption that he leaked it to the Slavic group. I told her to forget about it and downplayed the whole thing. When she was leaving, Annie said, 'I don't want it to seem that I'm asking for money, but can you get Msgr. Pat to pay my brother's funeral expenses? I don't have it.' I told her that Pat would take care of it.

"That's not all. Mrs. Robbins is in a nursing home in Ashville, North Carolina. Matilda Blaine had originally told me that it was in Raleigh, but she called my office with a new address. I'm going to see her two days from now. She doesn't know that I'm coming but we will wait and see how that all works out. Also, my investigator, big Jack Lecki, is on the case locating Johnny Blaine. So things are looking up. Keep the faith."

"Jim, why are you so intent on speaking to Ginny Robbins? She was the one who caused my conviction."

Jim said, "There had to be a reason why she lied at your trial, and more damaging was why she gave you the note two days before the murders." With that he left, saying he would be back soon.

Three hours later he was back. Chad asked, "Why are you back so soon? Did something happen to Pat?"

Jim answered, "He's all right, but something happened at the cathedral office. Annie Brown went to see Pat and became belligerent. She was very disturbed and made wild demands. Annie wanted one hundred thousand dollars because she said her brother died because of you and the detectives would be interested in hearing what she had to say about it. When Pat tried to calm her down, she reacted by pulling a gun out and yelling that he would have to be sacrificed in exchange for Chuck's death. Fortunately, he had left his speakerphone on and the receptionist heard everything. She called the police and me.

"When the police arrived, Pat had already taken the gun from her. She was crying hysterically and then blurted out to the police that you killed Iggy and her brother died because of you. Apparently, they reported this to the detectives working on the investigation and they contacted me. I rushed here to tell you that they were getting a warrant out to take your DNA. We'll fight it. They also said you're the principal suspect and will be bringing the case to a State Grand Jury. Then they made a stupid request—would you consent to a polygraph test? I told them no way as you are already facing execution in twenty-six days.

"Chad, they don't have a case. There are no witnesses, and her testimony is strictly hearsay. I have to leave now, but don't speak to anyone as they might want to catch you off guard."

He was speechless but managed to say, "I'll do whatever you say."

The next morning the warden asked that he come to his office. These same two detectives were there with a warrant to take his DNA. Chad refused and told them to contact his lawyer.

The younger one said, "We know you did it. Why don't you own up to it? You're going to die soon anyway."

Chad very calmly said," Fuck you," and turned to the warden and asked if he could return to his cell.

Walking back, Chad talked to himself. "Where am I going? Even if I beat the Robbins murders, I will still have to contend with Iggy's death."

He then smiled as he remembered what Irish had told him. "There were no witnesses, and Chuck's dead."

That night Chad had another nightmare. He and Jeri were lying together in a big coffin. They had just finished making love and now were sleeping peacefully. Mrs. Robbins had been watching them. She then wheeled her chair to the casket and said, "Wake up. I never wanted you two together, dead or alive."

CHAPTER 24

Pat and Irish came the next day and told him of the recent developments concerning Johnny Blaine.

Jim said, "My investigator, Big Jack, paid him a visit and was told that Johnny was an aide to Congressman Koski. He said that his cousin, Ginny, got him the job. He was reluctant to talk but realized he had a problem with what went on at your trial. My take was that he was angling for immunity, and that became a reality when he told Big Jack that he wanted his attorney and a prosecutor present when he told his story. I made the arrangement for them to meet at my office tomorrow and called Jim Corrigan, a state deputy attorney. I knew Jim from Widner Law School. Paul Gibson, Blaine's attorney, confirmed the meeting. This may be what we've been waiting for."

Pat came over and gave Chad a big hug and tearfully said, "Have faith, brother; it's going to work out for you."

After they left, Chad became hopeful that by Johnny Blaine spilling his guts, he was going to be saved from execution.

The next day Jim came earlier than Chad had expected. He wore a sad face and explained that Johnny had disappeared. "His lawyer called and said he couldn't find his client. I got Big Jack to pay his sister a visit. We caught a break when she thought that Jack was a business associate of her brother's and told him that Johnny took off with his live-in girlfriend to Atlantic City.

"The speculation was that Johnny wanted to get lost until after your execution. Jack contacted the Atlantic City police and explained the situation. They explored every hotel without any luck. They then caught a break when the Absecon police called and said they had his girlfriend, Monica, sitting in their headquarters. Jack and an Atlantic City detective headed there and were extremely successful in an interview with her.

"Monica told them of their night at the Taj Mahal Casino and how Johnny hit five numbers in a row at the Roulette table for fifty-five hundred dollars. She said, 'He was so giddy and began to drink a lot. So did I, but at some point I stopped. He didn't. Our car had been parked by the valet, and with the help of the attendant we were able to get him into the passenger's seat. He immediately passed out as I started to drive to the motel in Absecon.

"'I then decided to get him to a diner on Highway Thirty for some strong black coffee. I woke him up and force-fed him two big cups. Now he was semi-alert.

"'When we arrived at the motel, I helped him upstairs to the room. He insisted on opening the door with the key. That turned out to be a lucky break for me. Two masked men dragged him into the room and started to beat him up. I don't know if they didn't see me or weren't interested in me. All I know is that I ran to the car and drove to a 7-Eleven and called the police. They took me back to the room, where we found Johnny unconscious on the floor. He was bleeding profusely from the head. They took him to a local hospital and told me he was close to death. I never saw Johnny after that day.

"'The police asked me to come back and meet with you today, and here I am.' Monica also told the police that the two men were speaking in a foreign tongue, something like Polish or Russian. The police then told her to go back and visit with her mom in Ohio and gave her all the money they'd found in Johnny's pocket."

Chad was visibly disappointed, but Jim said there was good news as to Ginny Robbins.

"When I visited her, she was seated in a wheelchair staring into space. I tried talking to her, but there was no response or acknowledgment that I was in the room. After a half hour of nothing, I decided to talk to her aide. The woman was a forty-eight-year-old Haitian named Cora who spoke English. I asked her if Ginny was like this all the time, and she said no. I then asked if she talked, and Cora answered yes. I then asked if she makes sense when she talks, and again the answer was yes.

"That prompted me to slip her two one hundred-dollar bills so she would cooperate and requested she tell Ginny that I didn't buy her act and further, that I'm coming back with a deputy attorney general with a warrant for her arrest due to her fraudulent testimony at your trial. I was really bluffing because I didn't know how far my threat would go. When I left, I felt confident that we would be hearing from her. Upon arriving at my office, I called the attorney general, Jimmy Corrigan, and told him about Johnny Blaine and Ginny Robbins. I then asked him to get the governor to delay the execution. He immediately came back and said that the governor would need more definitive evidence.

"But my intuition was right about Ginny, because early this morning she sent a message that she wants to speak with your brother. So Pat is going there tomorrow and will wear a wire. If she only wants to talk, then that would be just fine. It becomes more complex if she wants him to hear her confession. Then your brother will need to make a decision whether to reveal what she tells him. Pat said if it meant saving your life, he would break his vow and leave the priesthood. We have to see how this all plays out."

Chad then told Jim, "Tell Pat to get her to talk rather than confess and to watch his back, because we don't know who is behind this conspiracy. It could be a trap. At this point I don't have much hope."

"Chad, it's going to be all right. I believe that this is a classic case of someone who wants to make peace with her maker." With that being said, he left Chad, who was wishing for a new tomorrow.

CHAPTER 25

P at was smiling from ear to ear when he walked into the warden's office two days later. Right then, Chad knew things were good. Pat couldn't control himself and yelled out, "I think we have a winner." He then began to cry as he hugged his younger brother.

Jim and Pat had traveled to the nursing home as planned, and they taped a wire to his chest in the men's room.

Pat described how he was totally surprised when he stepped into her room. She was sitting up in bed, all made up, looking like a fading movie star. He was caught off guard because of what Jim had told him about her mood and condition.

Ginny then told Pat, "It has been a long time. I'm so proud of what you have done with your life."

"Mrs. Robbins, it's been a long time, and I am here at your beck and call."

She said, "I want to make a confession to you, especially since it deals with your brother. However, I know you could not publicize it because of your vows. Therefore, I am releasing you from any priestly vow."

With that she handed him a notarized affidavit from a physician certifying she was of right mind and said, "It all began when my detective discovered your mother and my husband frequented the Winslow Motel. I confronted them both, only to hear them say they were in love. I felt so rejected because I thought I had the perfect marriage. From that moment on all I could think of was revenge. After a morning of heavy drinking, I met with your father at Café Olé. When he sat down, I could tell he was very nervous, as if he was anticipating the reason for our meeting. I told him about the affairs and showed him the photos. He didn't say much and left rather abruptly. Later that day I got the news that he killed your mother and himself.

"What happened caused me to despise my husband much more and set me on a course to destroy him. I could have lived with his cheating, but I could never forgive him for what he did to all of us. Then to top it all, he was faking such sorrow and eulogizing your father. What a joke. Because I was so intent on bringing him down, I actually forgot about my daughter. Thus, when Carl came into Jeri's life, I found myself confiding in him like the son I never had. Funny how I couldn't talk to my daughter, but because Carl was so sympathetic to me and eager to listen, he became a sounding board for me.

"Carl later introduced me to his uncle, George Koski. At the time he was chairman of special ethics groups for the election of President Garrett. My husband, Jamie, was the national chair of lawyers for Garrett. I was president of the Republican club in our town and eventually became an office staffer in the DC headquarters for the length of the campaign.

"George always dropped by to say hello and chat. One day he invited me to lunch and I accepted. Jamie was traveling a lot, so I wound up going to lunch with George a couple of times a week. I was definitely attracted to him and let him know it. I had not made love for a long time, and as a result, I couldn't suppress my sexual desires anymore. We graduated to a hotel room and began a long affair. George was a lover who satisfied me and made me feel like a woman again.

"During pillow talk George told me he had a plan that would achieve two goals. First he would convince President Garrett to appoint Jamie as ambassador to Gamba in the Middle East. He then would arrange to bring Carl and Jeri to live with us at the embassy. Secondly, there was a lot of money to be made by dealing with the Karners. He wanted Carl and me to get a piece of that money bank. He concluded by saying that Jamie would be so humiliated that he would need to resign. I joined George for revenge of Jamie but at the same time, I actually became a traitor to my country."

She then asked Pat if she could rest for an hour and if he could come back. Pat took the affidavit out to the waiting room and shared it with Jim. Together they read it and found it replete with admissions regarding false statements made by Ginny at the trial. She had admitted that she lied on the stand and that it was fixed with Judge Mary Bryant that her cousin Johnny Blaine become the jury foreman. Her affidavit stated that Chad was not the murderer but Gustave Koski and Ernie Jinks were. They were supposed to kill Jamie only and not harm Jeri at all.

Apparently, George changed the agreement not to harm Jeri when she became engaged to Chad. Ginny was lied to, and she would never forgive George because he took her only child.

After the murders, George became threatening and vowed to kill her if she did not go along with them. So she lied and cooperated in fear of her own life. The affidavit concluded that everything including her fears were now meaningless now that she had been diagnosed with terminal cancer only three days prior.

Upon reading the document, Jim immediately left for his office. He was excited and bent on filing an order to show cause with the Maryland State Supreme Court requesting that the judgment of conviction be dismissed and Chad be released immediately.

Meanwhile, Pat stayed around to hear her confession.

She said, "Before we were assigned to Gamba, the doctors diagnosed me with MS. Now I had more reason to hate because I couldn't bear the thought of being disabled. Upon our arrival at the embassy, Hadi was already in place and in charge. Somehow George had made the contact to infiltrate Hadi as director overseeing all nonmilitary personnel. However, his real role was to represent Karner, who in turn became the buyers of all classified documents and information. From inception we all underestimated Hadi, who in time came to rule us."

"Together, he and Sgt. Perry formed a very profitable side business of selling secrets, weapons, and illegal drugs to various government bases in the Middle East. We were all afraid of Hadi; he was creepy and nasty. That man ordered everyone around and was continually disrespectable to Americans, except for Sgt. Perry. I had very little to do with him and warned Carl to do the same. Carl said his uncle put him in that position for a reason. I told Carl that his uncle must not have known that this man was an animal.

"Things got worse when Carl confronted him and asked for a share of the money from the drug business. Hadi said he would let Carl's wife and mother-in-law live if Carl would bring classified documents to him.

Carl didn't realize how serious Hadi was until three hours later when he pushed me down the stairs. I was in my room resting when Hadi came with another servant, dragged me out of my chair, and flung me down the stairs. When my daughter and son-in-law came to my aid and asked Hadi what happened, he calmly said, 'Accidents do happen.' Fortunately, my injuries were not serious, but he made his point. From that moment on we were in constant fear for our lives. Carl began to cooperate with him.

"Frankly, I never saw any of the money passed onto George. I just assumed Carl took care of that. I didn't care about it since it was my intent to destroy Jamie. However, everything changed when Chad and Nellie showed up at the embassy. We then found out that Jamie had contacted the White House and accused Carl of being one of the betrayers.

"He had no clue that George and I had been involved. At that time I blamed Chad for Carl's death because he forced Hadi to take terroristic actions. George later visited me when we got back to the states. Jamie and Jeri were out and he came by the house. He wanted to make love but I couldn't chance it in my own house.

"George became livid and then said that Jamie and Chad must go. They know too much, plus they were responsible for Carl's death. He further said that if it were not for them, he would still be alive. Then he promised to kill them but would spared both my daughter's and my life only if we didn't betray him. That is when I said to him: 'But George, I thought you loved me, and now you're threatening me.' He answered, 'Ginny, I never loved you; you were my sex toy. The killing will not take place for a while, but you need to be part of the plan.'

"I was tricked into believing Jeri would not be harmed. Instead I witnessed both violent deaths as they kept stabbing and stabbing. All I could see was blood gushing from her body like a fountain. I cried out, and they started after me but got spooked when Chad pulled into the driveway. By this time I was backing into my room, and they had run out the backdoor. That is when I made my decision to save my own life as I saw Chad bending over and caressing my daughter's limp body. He was now the murderer. I also realized then that George had used me and had made me part of his conspiracy.

"After the trial, my cousin Matilda helped me to disappear to this area. Upon arriving here, I continually acted as if I had dementia. I spoke only to Cora and paid her well for her silence.

"George found out where I was and sent his goons here. But once they saw my condition, they backed off, convinced I would never to be able to tell my story. Pat, I've been afraid of dying, but now I don't give a damn. Tell Chad I'm sorry and that I love him."

CHAPTER 26

Jim showed up at the jail and was tremendously excited. He told Chad that after he filed the papers, the clerk called. The court had set a hearing for November 19, two days from now.

He said, "We have to prepare and review what is best needed on your behalf.

"I want to have Pat testify as to his conversation with Ginny, including the confession that she waived at the beginning of their time together. Also, we need her doctor present to testify as to her mental competence. I'll take care of that by flying him up and having my assistant babysit him. That's all for us. Meanwhile, the state is having a psychiatrist evaluate Ginny at this moment."

Chad then asked him, "What does this all mean?"

"If she is credible and understandable, you get to go home. Make sure you dress in your officer's uniform. See you there."

After he left, Chad felt like a new man. His life was about to be given back to him. The whole turn of events made him very nervous now that the Iggy matter was surfacing and thoughts of what kind of life he could ever have without Jeri.

The two days flew, and on the hearing date he was transported to the Supreme Court building in Baltimore. When he entered the courtroom, he could not help noticing the very austere and classical look of the room. The room itself was almost all mahogany and there were seven tall leather chairs behind the bench.

Pat was already there, smiling and looking very priestly in his red and black cassock. He was an awesome sight, and Chad could not believe that it was really happening to him. Jim came over to him and repeated for the tenth time not to intervene or say anything unless a question was directed at him.

Chad thought, *Something good is going to happen. Today is nineteen days before the execution.*

Precisely at 9:30 a.m., the clerk called the court into session and the seven black robed judges filed in.

Chief Justice Francis West started by saying, "This is the most unique set of circumstances that I have encountered in my twenty-seven years on the bench. Yesterday, we had to have a special conference to determine how we were going to address these new and revealing facts. It was decided that a hearing would be proper."

Turning to the court reporter, he said, "Please note for the record that Commander Braden is present. Mr. Brady, do you have any witnesses here?"

Jim said rather loudly, "Yes, Judge."

"Mr. Corrigan, how about you?"

"I only have one: Dr. John O'Toole, president of the University of Maryland and world-renowned psychiatrist."

"Mr. Brady, you are the moving party; call your witness."

"Thank you, Chief Justice. I call Dr. James Black to the stand."

Once sworn, the doctor explained that he'd spent several hours with Mrs. Robbins to determine her mental competency. He said he was satisfied with her results, and after fifteen leading questions from Jim, Dr. Black opined that she was and is of sound mind.

Next he called Msgr. Braden, who summarized Ginny's confession for the court. The Justices seemed satisfied with the information and announced that all questions would be reserved until after the state's witness, Dr. O'Toole, testified.

Chad's heart was fluttering not knowing what the doctor might say. As he was called, tensions were high and even the news media were on the edge of their seats.

Corrigan began to question him when the Chief Justice interrupted him and asked, "Counsel, do you mind if we asked the questions of Dr. O'Toole."

He was quick to say, "Of course not, Your Honor."

Justice Miriam Brown, way down at the end, then said, "Doctor, we are aware of your impeccable credentials and ask that your answers be simple. Did you perform an examination of Mrs. Robbins, and if so, where and when, and what is your opinion as to her mental competency at this time?"

"I examined her two days ago at the nursing home in North Carolina. She was alone in her room when I performed the perfunctory tests such as blood pressure, listening to her heart, etc. Other than her problems of getting around and suffering from stage 4 cancer, she was in a good frame of mind. I then gave her a series of mental exercises, both verbal and picture illustrative. The latter is a technique employed by myself throughout my many years of practice. It consists of displaying pictures to the patient of her home, childhood, death scene, and victims. It is meant to shock the patient into reality. Verbally she was asked about the nursing home, how long she had been there, the name of her doctor, the names of her nurses and aides, the names of her medications, her feelings about her condition, and then a focus on current events.

"She passed all the tests, and I was satisfied that Mrs. Robbins was aware of what was happening at this juncture. I also inquired about her confession to the monsignor, and she completely supported his version. The pictures were meant to flush out her hatred for her late husband. However, she broke down hysterically upon seeing a picture of her daughter, Jeri. She then said, 'Damn it, Lord, what did I do to my only child? I sentenced her to death.' Mrs. Robbins then said to me, 'Tell the world that Chad Braden is innocent. I was only following George Koski's orders in framing him. He had always swore that Chad was responsible for his beloved nephew's death.' The last thing she added was to make sure Chad was set free."

The Chief Justice then looked at the doctor and asked for his conclusion as to whether she was of a right mind and capable of understanding the nature of the statements she had made. Dr. O'Toole did not hesitate and answered in the affirmative.

At that moment Chad knew his ordeal was over.

The Justices met at a sidebar for a few minutes and then returned to their seats. Chief Justice West then asked Chad to stand and informed him that he was a free man and was released forthright. The courtroom erupted into cheers and grand applause.

Corrigan was instructed to arrest Judge Mary Bryant and Congressman George Koski for conspiracy and obstruction of justice.

Reporters gathered around Chad, but he refused to comment.

As they were leaving the courtroom, Jim said, "I don't want to burst your balloon, but Corrigan told me the Iggy case is going to the Grand Jury next week."

CHAPTER 27

It was eight in the morning, and Chad was sitting in Captain Kondrak's office awaiting further orders. Kondrak was late because of an emergency. Chad was daydreaming and reliving the last seven glorious days. They were like a blur. Irish Jim had arranged to get him a luxurious condo in Arlington, mainly to give him space from the media.

He was alone at the condo when Pat called, telling him that a surprise package was being delivered within a half hour. When the doorbell rang, Chad rushed to answer it with a high sense of anxiety. There was his old girlfriend, Sherry, with a major grin on her face, singing "Happy Birthday." She came in, kissed him, and threw open her raincoat. Her big boobs were bouncing up and down; she was totally naked. Sherry had been writing him letters and now was totally back in his life. Chad had been taken aback by the intellect displayed in her letters. Now, seeing her in person, he could not get over how great she looked. From the time that he had last seen her, she had gone to modeling school, studied the business, and moved over to sales, where she became the top producer for the Blush product line. Sherry admitted to having several boyfriends over the course of years but said she always loved Chad. He was overcome with emotion.

The next three days consisted of endless lovemaking, a variety of takeout orders, and plenty of TV. Sherry was sexually better than ever. The exercise was just what he needed to bring him down to earth. But most of all, he saw a different side of her that emerged from some serious conversations between encounters.

She confessed that she had been forever waiting for him and said, "There was never anyone else for me."

He didn't know what to say, reluctant to make any commitment at this juncture, but he also didn't turn her away.

TV covered the arrests of George Koski and Judge Mary Bryant for several days. Chad was delighted to see that the coverage extended to the Capitol, where Koski was taken into custody. The arrest of the judge was even more melodramatic as the police marched into her courtroom during a trial and asked her to step down from the bench. She was disrobed and handcuffed prior to being taken to jail. Such a fitting ending to a glorious career. Not unexpectedly, both were out of jail on bail within twenty-four hours.

The captain then came into the room and interrupted Chad's reverie. "After your call, we've been able to trace the whereabouts of Gustave Koski and Ernie Jinks. We think they're hiding in a small West Virginia mountain town called Locust. I have taken the liberty of reaching out for your old friend Captain Spud and his men. They will be meeting you in three days at a village called Adelphia. There is a small airport there, and Locust is only an hour drive away. Is there anything else that you need for me to do?"

Chad asked about a plan, and Captain Kondrak said that there would be equipment, vehicles, and firepower in the locked hangar at the airport under guard. He also told Chad that he would be transported by helicopter from National about four in the morning. Finally he gave Chad a sealed envelope to be shared with Spud.

Chad thanked the captain and asked if he could see Nellie the next day and would he arrange it. The response was an immediate yes, and provisions would be made for a small flight to Westchester Airport and a private car to the hospital.

Spring was in the air as Chad was driving to National and the plane to Westchester. He was somewhat concerned as he didn't know what to expect of Nellie, and was she aware of his recent problems. He landed at Westchester and went to a government car.

The drive was about an hour long, and Chad relived in his mind the tragic circumstances regarding Nellie. She had been so vibrant and full of life, and God only knew what she was now. He felt sleepy because the sun was beating down on him. It was very warm in the car, almost as if the air conditioning was not operating. He couldn't wait to get out of that hotbox.

When they arrived at the hospital, he was able to see Nellie from a distance sitting on the veranda.

Chad approached her and noted she was neatly dressed and that her hair was made up. She almost looked like her old self. When he got closer, he noticed she was sleeping.

Finally she looked up and said, "Chad, is that you? The media had you long gone and here you are. I'm excited to see you. Please tell me all."

He was taken aback by her speech and demeanor. "Nellie, I'm so happy to see you like this. Of course I'll tell you everything. Are you able to walk?"

They started to walk to the green area behind the building.

Chad told her everything—how they knew who the real killers were, where they were hiding in the Blue Ridge Mountains in a town called Locust, and how they would be getting them with the aid of Captain Spud. He also told her of the plan and noticed that she was listening intensely.

She said, "The plan sounds like it might work."

After they finished the walk, she asked if they could go for a ride. She and Chad sat in the backseat, and the driver gave them privacy. Nellie asked Chad if he could hold her hand and she snuggled close to him. The ride lasted about an hour and a half, and upon their return, she asked if he could stay for a couple more hours. When he said yes, Nellie invited him to her room.

The hospital had been recently renovated, resulting in her room being quite large and airy. The flowers in the sitting room had all the appearances of a modern suite at a hotel. Actually, she had all the comforts, including a twenty-six-inch Sony TV.

They entered the room, and Nellie turned to Chad and asked to be kissed, which started a flurry of passion between them. She felt his erection and suggested the door be locked and that they go to the bed. He wasn't prepared for all of that, but after years of trying to get to that point with her, it made him more anxious and excited. She then proceeded to take off her clothes without hesitation. He was astonished at how beautiful her body was; it was just as he had envisioned it over the many years he had yearned for her. She then asked him to make love to her. He was amazed how good she was in bed.

When they were done, Nellie continued to kiss him and stroke his hair. Meanwhile, Chad was kind of silent and confused, because he had always wanted Nellie and now he had two women in his life.

As he was leaving, Nellie said, "Chad, will you come back for me""

"I promised once that we could make a life together, so maybe it's still possible."

Flying home, he was on an emotional high and was thoroughly convinced that Nellie was now all right. He had asked her about the big improvement, and she said rather simply, "Shock treatments."

Nellie was looking out the window trying to catch a glimpse of Chad's car leaving the parking area. Upon affirming that the car had left, she asked the head nurse for permission to make a long distance phone call.

"George, you paid me $250,000 for the information that went into the botched bombing in London, and then another $250,000 for working with Hadi, and he almost killed me. Now I have the details as to how they want to get your son, and it's going to cost you another half a million dollars. I want the cash deposited the same way into my Swiss account. Once I know the money is there, I'll give you the details of the plan. You'd better hurry, because they intend to take action in two days. You're lucky Chad paid me a surprise visit or your son would be a dead man."

George responded, "Thanks, Nellie. The money will be in your account within an hour, just like the other times. Call me back with the plan."

CHAPTER 28

Two days later Chad was waiting at the Adelphia Airport for Spud and his crew. They were late, and Chad decided to go over to the hangar where the captain had said that the equipment for the mission would be stored. Once inside, he was able to observe two black Hummers parked next to each other. As he approached the cars, a number of gunshots caused him to hit the ground and take cover.

He then crawled to where the equipment was and helped himself to a Thompson machine gun and plenty of ammunition. He was now able to return fire, and this saved his life. Spud and his men rushed into the hangar to join the fight. When the firing came to a halt, they were able to determine that two invaders were dead, but at least two others got away. They took off in a SUV parked outside the back of the hangar and were seen driving on the small road leading to the mountain highway.

Chad and Spud jumped into one Hummer and tried to catch them. Meanwhile, Spud's Rangers jumped into the other Hummer and followed their leader. Chad's heart was pumping in reaction as to how Spud was driving. This became evident when they hit a bump or came close to the mountain edge. The second Hummer was about a mile behind them because they'd paused to pick up the fallen equipment.

They were close to the top of the mountain when Spud looked into the rearview mirror and said, "Chad, we're being followed by a black van, and it's not my men."

He then called the other Marines and asked them to intercept this vehicle. At that moment, Chad realized he had told Nellie the plan and no one else knew. He then sadly surmised that she was part of the plot to kill him. He couldn't believe it, but it was the truth.

The black van closed in on them and then rammed their vehicle. Immediately Spud accelerated his speed in an attempt to get away. Again, the van rammed their Hummer. It was obvious that they were trying to push them off the road and down the cliff.

Spud then turned to Chad and yelled," Hold on!" He put his foot down on the gas all the way, causing the Hummer to lurch forward, and while doing so, he hit the brakes while turning to the right. This caused the van to crash into the right rear of the Hummer and bounce back, where it was hit by the trailing Marine vehicle. The van caromed off the rail and went off the road and down the mountain to a blazing destruction. The occupants were unknown as there was never a real visual of the two.

Luckily their Hummer, though badly damaged, had managed to stay on the road. Other than some minor cuts and bruises, Spud and Chad were intact.

The second Hummer also sustained heavy damage, but everyone was okay.

Chad invented a plan. "It's apparent that Gustav and Ernie's bodies are burned, but we need to recover what's left of their remains and put them on ice for a while. Have the navy issue a report that attackers got away and their whereabouts are unknown at this time. It would not be surprising that they have left the country. Further, the bodies of Chad Braden and Captain Spud Turner were burned in the fiery wreckage that occurred when their vehicle went airborne down the mountain."

Five days later it was pouring rain as the mourners stood at Chad's gravesite in Arlington Cemetery. The sky was very dark and it was only ten in the morning. Pat Braden, Captain Kondrak, and Nellie were among many mourners. They were staring down at the hole in the ground and the flag-draped casket bearing Chad's remains. They had informed Sherry of the plot, so she was not present.

The private service lasted about twenty minutes. Most notable was the eulogy by Msgr. Pat. He concluded by saying, "I can remember vividly when my brother told me that he had only nineteen days to execution. He was obsessed with the countdown and felt he was clinging to life by a thread. Fortunately he was released, but it was God's will that he never made it past that nineteen-day mark. Because, you see, today is the nineteenth day. His was a life marred by tragedies—first, our parents, and then what happened to Nellie, and then the murder of Jeri. I recall him saying that maybe now was the time for a normal life with Nellie.

"Again, it wasn't meant to be. Rest in peace, dear brother."

Nellie, dressed in sheer black with a long veil, approached the coffin and placed the first rose on the draped casket. As she was saying her good-bye, she sobbed loudly and had trouble maintaining her balance. Pat. took her by the shoulders and helped her away. Then all the others followed in line and retreated to an area where they could witness the coffin being lowered into the ground.

A limousine pulled up the road by the gravesite, and they commenced their two-hour ride to the rectory at the Sacred Heart Cathedral in Baltimore.

The occupants had very little conversation on their long and somber drive.

Upon arriving, Pat suggested to Nellie that she should go to her room and rest before dinner at four. She nodded and left. All the others retired to the library for drinks and conversation.

At four she came down, looking very refreshed and calm. They went into this very austere-looking room with a high ceiling, two large chandeliers, a long dining table, and large, dark-red chairs.

Nellie sat next to Pat at the head of the table. There was a lot of small talk for about five minutes—interrupted by Chad, very much alive and dressed in his navy blues, who walked into the room and went directly to Nellie.

Everyone was dumbfounded, as only his brother was privy to the staged funeral.

Nellie cried out, "Oh my God," and began to cry hysterically.

Chad calmly said to her, "I knew it was you when they first tried to get me at the hangar and the mountain road. You were the only person that I told of our plan to get Gustav and Ernie. Then it hit me like a brick. It was you all along. You knew where my office was in London and coincidentally, the explosion happened a week before you showed up. I also figured that you tipped Hadi about the raid and then faked the kidnapping, the rape, and the hostage scenario. All this time you've been manipulating the doctors, nurses, and everyone else about your condition. Why, Nellie, you knew that I loved you and you played me all these years. We were lucky that it was Gustav and Ernie that went down the mountain instead of us. Why? Why, Nellie!"

She stopped crying, and with her voice trembling, said, "There were a million reasons—and that is what George paid me to get you." Nellie then reached into her pocket, and before anyone could stop her, put a suicide pill into her mouth.

Chad vaulted the table and tried to wrench the pill from her mouth. But he was too late; she had already swallowed it.

Nellie fell to the floor and began to convulse. Chad knelt next to her face. She whispered something and then lost consciousness. Nellie died on the way to Baltimore Memorial Hospital.

Chad was with her to the end. After spending hours with the police, he returned to the rectory.

Msgr. Pat asked what Nellie had whispered.

Chad answered, "She said, 'I will always love you.'"

CHAPTER 29

A month had passed when Irish Jim called and gave Chad more bad news. He said, "Corrigan called and was thinking of proceeding to the Grand Jury on the Iggy killing. He wanted you to know you were the target of that investigation. It appears that other than Chuck's sister, who is now unstable, an independent witness has surfaced, a guy called Mario Henderson. Supposedly he was passing by the shower area and saw you emerge just before they discovered Iggy's body."

Chad asked, "How come this witness surfaces just now? The safe bet is that Iggy's men planted him to get me."

"That's what Corrigan thinks and is giving you the benefit of the doubt while he investigates this Mario guy. Meanwhile, we'll play the waiting game. I'll keep in touch."

That very same day news broke that the congressman's criminal case had been assigned for trial to Judge David Platt of the Federal District Court in Greenbelt, Maryland. His attorneys had brought motions before the court to dismiss the charges or, in the alternative, reduce them to a lesser degree. They were all denied.

The trial started a couple of weeks later. The publicity was overwhelming, and there was talk that the government was contemplating implicating his wife, Sylvia. A leak of part of the government's case indicated that there was proof that she had visited Nellie on four different occasions and further opened a Swiss bank account for Nellie. Oddly, the government backed away from that strategy for an unknown reason.

The courthouse in Greenbelt was new and pristine. On the first day of jury selection, the courtroom was filled with an overflow of media.

After all, this was the famous George Koski. Judge Platt preached to everyone that this was going to be a fair trial, not a circus. Chad had been subpoenaed as the stellar witness for the government. He was the only remaining witness, as Nellie was dead and Ginny was in a coma.

Johnny Blaine was not available since he was now a living vegetable resulting from the beating at the hands of Koski's henchman.

Two things happened as Chad started to testify. His old friend Kit came into the courtroom and sat right next to Sherry. She was there to lend moral support and could become a hostage in waiting. Secondly, Koski's attorney made a motion to exclude everything Nellie had told him on her deathbed. He claimed that it was all hearsay. The US attorney argued that a deathbed confession was outside of the hearsay rule and should be admitted. The other side then argued that the confession was before she took the suicide pill and thus was not a deathbed confession. In a surprise ruling, the judge found for Koski on this issue and asked the government if it had any other witness ready to testify. He answered that because of the ruling, it had no other witness available at this time and requested a two-week adjournment. The court would only give one week before the case was dismissed with prejudice.

The ruling made great media news and favored the congressman by deeming him a victim of a witch hunt. Kit had disappeared from the courtroom when the judge made his decision. Chad asked Sherry if that man who sat next to her had anything to say. She said no and wondered why he'd asked. Eventually, Koski was never tried and all charges were dismissed. The explanation was that the case was severely weakened and thus they chose to wait for another day.

Sherry and Chad decided to get serious about their relationship. They were now hot and heavy into their romance. Both were extremely happy and planned to wed once the Iggy problem went away. Chad asked Sherry to give up her career and trade it for a family. She jumped at the suggestion and said hey would have a great time making babies. Chad then decided to push the button with Irish Jim and asked that Jack try to get to the bottom of this surprise witness, Mario Henderson. The next day they all met, and Jack promised to have results within hours.

True to his promise, Jack called Irish within a couple of hours and requested a meeting.

Jack said, "Mario Henderson is a slight young Negro punk who was being sexually abused by his fellow prisoners. He's doing hard time because of a failed armed robbery attempt at a major bank. He was backing out of the bank with the bag of cash in one hand and a shotgun in the other when he stumbled. That caused him to shoot his right thumb off, and when they caught him, the match was made with recovered thumb with his right hand. I met with my contact who told me that he has been adopted and protected by a Russian called Bresnak. The Russian got his punk, and the punk got his protector. Bresnak is the leader of the gang who is intent on avenging Iggy by getting Chad."

Irish asked the state to give Mario a polygraph test to determine the veracity of his anticipated testimony. Before that could take place, Henderson folded and gave up Bresnak. All he asked was to be transferred to another prison. Concurrently, the warden was asked to break up that gang by making wholesale transfers of the members. Bresnak was dealt with individually, transferred, and placed in solitary.

Two weeks later the press reported that Congressman Koski had suffered a massive heart attack and was not expected to recover. He died within twelve hours of the announcement.

Chad wanted to believe that his problems were over but was naturally apprehensive because of his history. He feared the next strike against him and his loved ones. He also didn't buy Koski's death. He felt it was too coincidental.

CHAPTER 30

Two years later Chad and Sherry were at the cathedral for the baptism of their firstborn, Mark Patrick Braden. It was October 19, and a very dark and windy day. The families had arrived at twelve thirty for the one o'clock ceremony. The church was empty except for them. The chosen godparents were Irish Jim and Sherry's sister, Joan.

When it was five minutes to one and Msgr. Pat had not shown, Chad became rather leery and decided to look for him. He was headed to the sacristy when he encountered the altar boy holding his bleeding head. He kept screaming, "They are killing the monsignor!"

As Chad ran into the room, he saw two figures dressed in black running out the rear exit. He was able to observe that one assailant was a well-built male and the other appeared to be a female.

His brother was on the floor. Pat had been stabbed several times in the upper arm and chest.

Chad tried to stop the bleeding by using his belt as a tourniquet and called out to the others to get help. Within minutes the police and paramedics were at the church. While riding in the ambulance with his brother, he surmised that the attack was intended to pick off his family members. He called Captain Kondrak and asked that Sherry, the baby, and her family be provided security until the danger passed.

Pat was unconsciousness for a day and a half. Chad had been by his side the entire time. When he woke, he told Chad that he was putting his vestments on when there was a noise behind him. He turned and saw Christian, the altar boy, being hit on the head by a person dressed in black. Then Pat was attacked by another person dressed in black.

Pat then asked his brother if he knew who they were and why now, after Chad's enemies had supposedly been eliminated. Before he could answer his brother, the doctor came in and shooed Chad from the room.

*

It was eight in the morning, and the Cathedral was packed with parishioners praying for the monsignor's recovery.

As he knelt, he couldn't dismiss from his mind the nightmare he'd had the night before. It was the same lady whose face he could not distinguish. She was telling him that someone close to him was going to be badly hurt. It had happened just as she'd promised, and now Chad was very concerned as to who may be the next target.

When he got home, reality and depression set in; his family was isolated from him. Pat was in the hospital, and so many people close to him had died tragically because of a special relationship with him. All these thoughts invaded his mind and were demons haunting him every moment of the day.

As the days passed, he was having trouble sleeping and concentrating on the problem confronting him and his loved ones. Over the course of two weeks he had lost fifteen pounds and had refused to leave the house for medical attention.

There were scary moments when he felt that all would be safe if he were out of the picture. One time, he took out his service revolver and placed it on the table. He kept staring and studying the gun before removing it to the weapon drawer, now safely secured.

Captain Kondrak paid him a visit and insisted he get medical help. He tried to convince him by mentioning that his family was terribly concerned and that the academy was with him all the way.

"I'm ordering you to see Captain Turner, navy psychiatrist, tomorrow."

Chad agreed and visited the doctor the next day. He was relieved when the doctor told him that his troubles were brought on by Chad having to fight a new war every other day. Adding to his anxiety was the fact that people were dying around him. Dr. Turner then prescribed an antidepressant and sleep medication and promised that within a four or five days, he would be back to his normal self.

Chad asked, "What happens if it doesn't work out that way?"

The answer from the good doctor: "Shock treatments."

That he didn't like.

Sure enough, after five days, he felt good. He was ready to go back to work and was upbeat about getting his family back home. Captain Kondrak had suggested that they could return but only with twenty four hour provided with guard. Chad asked that his brother be given security also. After a couple of normal days, Chad met with the local police and Naval Intelligence.

They had been busy investigating Pat's incident and were fortunate to come away with DNA from the altar boy's nails. He had fought back and was successful in scratching his attacker before being struck in the head.

Chad recognized her from a photo from that he had seen previously from that Irish Jim had received from the private investigator, Jack. She was the woman who had been with Johnny Blaine when he was beaten to a pulp.

Her name was Monica Paglia and had been allowed to return to Ohio with five thousand dollars of Johnny's money. Chad was told that the original detectives took her to an abandoned garage and, in exchange for a round of oral sex, released her. Another police officer turned them in when he overheard Monica offered to take care of them orally if they would give her the money.

The two new detectives were able to trace her to her mother's house in Niles, Ohio. Together with Chad, they boarded a private flight to Cleveland and drove to a quaint town with very old houses and stores. They found Mrs. Paglia's house without any problem. It was a single-family home that seemed to be at least one hundred years old.

Mrs. Paglia was a very pleasant woman of about seventy years old. Her husband had died in a train wreck many years ago. Once inside the house, they were astounded by the large number of religious statutes in the kitchen and living room. She readily told them she didn't know where Monica was now. When they told her of the attack on the monsignor, she made the sign of the cross and uttered, "Oh my God."

Mrs. Paglia then volunteered that Monica had been living with her and working part time at a local beauty salon as a hairdresser. Monica had let herself go and had gained a lot of weight.

She went on to say that Monica was always talking to her boyfriend by phone and never really told her who he was or where he lived. Then one day Monica told her mother that her boyfriend, Kit, was coming to visit her. She asked her Mom if there was any objection to him staying with them. Mrs. Paglia said she had none and was happy that at least Monica had a relationship. It wasn't long after that Kit, a giant of a man, showed up. Right from the outset, he was rude to Monica and Mrs. Paglia.

Mrs. Paglia then told the detectives and Chad what Kit said. "He said, 'Listen old lady, don't you bother us while I'm here. All you need to do is cook and leave us alone.' It was a hell of an introduction, and when my Monica said, 'She's all right,' Kit grabbed her and said, 'Don't ever question me—understand?' Monica nodded and they went upstairs. They were upstairs for two whole days. When Monica would come down for food, she would say to me, 'Mom, he is really good to me.' I answered, 'You're crazy, and I want both of you out of here.' They left that morning about two in the morning. Monica was always a strange girl."

It was then that Chad realized that Kit posed a danger to him and needed to be apprehended. But first they had to be found. The mother had no idea where they might have gone. It was also obvious that Monica was key in getting to Kit.

As they left, Chad said to Mrs. Paglia, "Your daughter is in big trouble, but we can help her. If she calls, tell her to call me. Here's my card." They left, never expecting to hear from her again.

CHAPTER 31

CHAPTER 31

C had was totally surprised when Anna Paglia called and said Monica had contacted her. She was living in College Park, Maryland, and Anna gave him the specific address. He immediately contacted the two detectives who had been working with him on this investigation. They decided to stake out the property, hoping to confront Monica. They sat in two separate cars about a half a block from the house and waited for a sign of Monica and Kit.

The house was like a mansion, set back with a long driveway, which appeared to be the only way in and out.

After a few hours on the second day of the surveillance, Kit emerged driving a black late-model Cadillac. He was alone and returned a couple of hours later. It had been agreed not to follow him and instead wait for Monica to come out. Later, they both left the house and drove to a nearby strip mall. Kit went into a liquor store, and Monica remained in the car.

Observing that she was alone, the two detectives snatched her from the car and left the area.

They brought her to the nearest police station and placed her in the interrogation room. All were taken aback in the change of her appearance. Her early photos displayed a beautiful young lady. Her present appearance was completely opposite. Her lipstick was smudged, the eyeliner application was heavy, her bleached hair was straggly, and a low-cut blouse exposed her big breasts and a fat, protruding stomach.

For a long time she refused to cooperate, but that came to an end when Chad informed her that they knew she had attacked the altar boy from her obtained DNA. He also told her they knew it was Kit who beat Msgr. Pat and that she was working for someone when Johnny Blaine was attacked.

Chad said, "Lady, you're staring at a long prison stay, but if you tell us what you know, we'll arrange it so you may never see the inside of a cell."

Her response was, "I want a lawyer to put this all down in writing before I give you the information. Plus, I'll need protection as they will definitely come after me."

One of the detectives said, "Who are 'they'?"

Monica calmly said, "I'll tell you when my lawyer tells me it's okay."

Monica was then driven to a headquarters in Baltimore where a public defender and a prosecutor were waiting. Chad could not erase from his mind the prior image of Monica as opposed to now. She was a stunning model type. Forty pounds heavier made a big difference. Her boobs were swollen and her tight rear end was now a big ass.

When they arrived, a public defender named Steve Panther requested to talk to Monica alone, and thirty minutes later he emerged saying the paperwork had to be done before Monica would give the information.

One hour later she was given the green light and started to spill everything. "I know who you are, Chad. Kit told me everything. The family wanted you so badly that they paid me fifty thousand to set up Johnny so that he could never testify for you. They wanted to see you executed and vowed to kill your family members. That is why the monsignor was chosen as a target.

"The plan was to gun you down when you came searching for your brother. Fortunately for you, that stupid altar boy screwed things up when he spotted us and began to yell. I put my hands around his throat and he scratched me. That's when Kit hit him over the head, and we ran out of the room through the back door, not knowing whether the monsignor was dead or alive. Later we heard on the news that he had survived."

Chad then asked her who was behind this whole plot against him, recognizing that Kit was not mentally capable of this work.

Monica responded. "It's the Russian mob. You became a target from the days that Kit and Ernie were working drugs for the family at the school. Then, when Carl was killed, that added fuel to their fire, followed by Iggy's death, a close relative, they figured it was you again. The last straw was when you hunted down and killed Gustav and Ernie. Now more than ever, and at any cost, they want you and your family dead."

"But I thought it all ended with the death of George Koski?"

"George was only a figurehead and reduced to nothing. He was killed because it was feared that he would soon crack."

"So then it wasn't a massive heart attack."

Monica explained that a private doctor had induced the heart attack. She went on to name Sylvia as the leader. "They were screwing while I was in Ohio and then right in front of me here while we were all living together. Sylvia is wicked and dangerous. She threatened to kill me if I didn't follow orders. I'm glad you caught me because it may have saved my life."

Chad said if the situation was so bad, why did they allow her to leave?

"Because they figured that I would never squeal."

Monica said Sylvia was from an elite Communist family who hated the United States and would do anything to harm Americans. She explained that Sylvia controlled the mob from the beginning and her marriage to George Koski was a way to infiltrate the government.

When asked where Sylvia and Kit were now, she replied, "At the big farmhouse guarded by two at the gate, two around the outside, and brute of a personal bodyguard in the house. He stays on the first floor, and they spend all their time in a recreation room and the bedroom."

Having said that, she began to cry hysterically and requested to rest. She was then taken to a safe house under police protection. Police were also sent to her mother's house in Ohio, fearing for her safety also.

A female officer took Monica to a safe house located about five miles away. The apartment was a dump, and the plan was to keep her there overnight until another location was secured. There was some pizza and soda, so the two ate and became friendly. The officer allowed Monica to call her mother and explain what was happening, but it appeared that her mom wanted no part of her, and she abruptly hung up.

Monica called her back and feigned that she was talking to her, but it was Kit on the other end of the line. The guard caught on and tried to restrain her but was overwhelmed by the heavier Monica. She kicked the guard in the stomach. As the officer curled up, Monica took her gun and pistol-whipped her about the head and face. The guard was then put in handcuffs while bleeding profusely from her injuries. Monica next called headquarters and said she had the guard as a hostage. She wanted Chad to come to the safe house.

Forty minutes later he pulled up to the safe house. His car was the only one on the lonely cul-de-sac. Before leaving headquarters, the detectives had put a tracking device on the undercarriage of the vehicle.

Monica opened the door holding the gun in one hand and motioning for him to put the wounded guard in the backseat of his car. The officer was having a difficult time breathing.

Monica then got into the passenger seat still holding the gun on Chad and instructed him to go to the Reagan National Airport, parking lot section C. She said, "There you will exchange her for my freedom."

While driving, Chad tried to dissuade Monica by saying that what she was doing was foolish because by cooperating, she could have been absolved of all crimes. Her told him to shut up and drive. He kept reminding her that if the officer died, she would be exposed to a murder charge. Again she told him to shut up. Chad felt that he was being led into a trap.

A half hour later Monica said, "There's his black van. Drive toward it and stop when I say so."

Chad was looking around for unmarked cars but saw none. Monica then yelled for him to stop and he did. He observed Sylvia and Kit walking toward him with their guns drawn.

Monica yelled, "Chad, get out of here!" She jumped out and shot them both at point-blank range. They were dead before having a chance to react to Monica. She then put the gun in her mouth and pulled the trigger.

It was all over, and Chad let out a tremendous sigh of relief. He called Captain Kondrak and asked him to bring his family back. Later that night they were all reunited: Sherry, the baby, the monsignor, and Chad. They celebrated knowing they were no longer in danger. All their enemies had been eliminated in one way or the other.

Amazingly, that night, he had the same haunting dream. This time he made out the face of the witch, and it was his mother. She said, "Don't worry; you can rest assured that there will not be any more attempts against you and your family."

He took this as sign of peace and was very happy that the woman was his mother. The nightmare had been put to rest.

Or so he thought.

CHAPTER 32

It was Sunday. Mark Braden and his sister, Edie, were at their father's bedside at the Baltimore Memorial Hospital. Their mother, Sherry, had passed two years ago from breast cancer.

Now their dad, Admiral Chad Braden. was suffering from the signs of a stroke. His speech was somewhat slurred, and his mouth was a little twisted. The doctors had scheduled a series of tests, and he seemed to be resting comfortably.

Both children had been at the hospital for at least six hours and took advantage of Chad dozing to visit the cafeteria. When they returned an hour later, he was not in the room. They encountered a policeman who told them an unknown assailant had stabbed Chad in the stomach several times. He was now undergoing emergency surgery. The attacker was apparently spooked by noise outside the door before he could complete his attack. He was then subdued by security and taken away.

The admiral was in surgery for five hours. Meanwhile, the whole family appeared: Mark's wife, June; his daughter, Sherry Ann; Edie's husband, Dr. John Rutter; his father, US Senator Mike Rutter; and newly appointed, Archbishop Braden.

Dr. Quinn appeared and said the admiral had made it through the surgery and would be in a rehab for at least a couple of weeks. They were able to see him, but he could not respond as was in a semi-coma state.

While Chad was in his coma, his brain was active to the extent of thinking about his children and their welfare. Interestingly enough, both children had fulfilled educational and family goals. Mark met June at Immaculate High School in nearby Annapolis. They both played clarinet and sat next to each other in band. Her father, Jim Doran, was the music teacher and convinced Mark to play alto saxophone. From that point the romance blossomed. While in school they had agreed not to have sex but did engage in heavy petting at times. After graduation, they both received scholarships to famed Juilliard School in Manhattan. Together they moved into an apartment on Fourteenth Street.

Mark met famous musician David Janks, who invited him to tour with his group in Europe. It was a great experience, until that night in Marseilles when a fire broke out and pandemonium erupted. They were lucky to get out through a side door backstage; however, fifty people died. The police investigated it as arson, but it led nowhere. There was speculation that it was radicals behind it, and Mark thought it strange that it was the same strain of terrorists that had pursued his father and failed.

They returned home and got married. June assumed her father's position at Immaculate High School, and Mark became the assistant bandmaster at Ocean Academy.

One year later, Sherry Ann was born.

Edie, the younger child, went to Georgetown and met John Rutter. He was the son of Senator Mike Rutter, who was well known as a strong prolife advocate.

Both Edie and John went on to medical school and were presently serving their residency at Mercy Hospital in DC. Their wedding was a small affair and only two months old when Chad got sick. Less than a month after their honeymoon, John had been working in the emergency room and left rather late one night. Upon entering the parking lot, he observed that there was no security as other nights. He thought that was rather strange. As he got to his car, he was hit on the head and dragged to a van.

He was bleeding from the wound, and his assailants gave him a towel. John was told to be quiet and that he would not be harmed.

When he asked, "Why me?," they told him it was because he was the son-in-law. The kidnappers rode around for ten hours. John didn't know if they were going to beat or kill him.

After the news announced that the senator's son was missing, they changed their plans. Now they were fearful of FBI involvement and decided to release him. He was dropped off at the Mayflower Hotel that afternoon.

Two days after Chad's surgery, Mark was on an academy bus with the band heading to Richmond, Virginia, for a basketball game. They were about two miles from their destination when an explosion occurred at the back of the bus. Fortunately, only the instruments were there and no lives were lost, although some band members were injured. Mark decided that this incident was no coincidence and that his whole family was at risk.

Senator Mike called a family meeting and said they could not wait any longer for protective security to save them from further harm. He made his point that whoever these people were, that they were out there to destroy the Braden family.

"These people intend to pick you off, one by one. I've asked the FBI and naval intelligence to get involved. We've decided it will be best to put you all into witness protection until the threat is eliminated. As for your dad, I'll keep a vigil over him and get you daily news under a form of security conversation."

Mark looked around and said, "The senator is right."

Edie softly uttered, "I don't want to leave Dad like this. Suppose something happens? How are we going to help him?"

The senator assured her that she must think about herself and John now. "I know the admiral would want it that way."

CHAPTER 33

Mark and his family were now the Sullivans and had been relocated to Tulsa, Oklahoma. Mark was Jack, June was Jenny, and their child was Rose. They were immediately plugged into the community by the government. Jack was now a high school music teacher, and Jenny was a teacher at the Lawrence School, which Rose attended.

Edie and her husband were now the Rankins and had relocated to Fort Worth, Texas. Edie was now Mary Ann and John was Jason. They became part of a low-income medical service under the auspices of the American Red Cross.

Two weeks after the relocation, Chad regained consciousness. Senator Mike was the only person in the room at the time. Chad asked about his family, and Mike explained that they had to be relocated for their safety.

"I'm the only person outside of the agency who knows where they are, and until we solve what and who is behind these attacks, they need to remain in the program."

"Okay, maybe I should do away with myself so the kids can live in peace—but on the other hand, I would like to get my hands on those bastards myself and blow them into infinity."

Mike informed him that he was being sent to rehabilitation section of the Naval Hospital located in Salem, Mass. He would be staying in a cottage by the ocean with a fulltime nurse and two FBI agents guarding the exterior. He was also advised that after three months, a plan would be put together to reunite him with his family.

The ambulance ride to Salem took about ten hours. Nurse Marge Felton was with him, and two agents followed in a separate car. Upon arrival they were directed to a cottage by the oceanfront. In actuality it was a large house consisting of five bedrooms, four bathrooms, a large kitchen, dining room, two studies, and a grand living room. It was rumored that several US presidents had vacationed there. Thus, the road to recovery was to begin for Chad.

Nurse Marge Felton was a very attractive woman of fifty-five and well qualified to take care of the admiral. Every day she would give him physical therapy and massages for about two hours. He would then rest for four hours and therapy would resume.

Marge was a very outgoing person whom he came to like very much. Chad appreciated the fact that she enjoyed having conversations with him on any subject and was in addition a very caring person. At night, they ate dinner and then spent some time on the grand porch facing the ocean. She then helped him to bed and gave him his nighttime medication and a sleeping pill. He came to rely on her very much and found it difficult to move around without her assistance.

After a couple of weeks their relationship was so intense that it blossomed into an intimate one. During the course of a massage, whether deliberately or not, she caused him to be aroused. She noticed it, and he was embarrassed.

Later that night Chad thought about it and concluded that she intentionally caressed him, causing his erection. When she came in to give his medication, he reached out for her and pulled her into bed. She appreciated the move, and they consummated the act. This would happen on other occasions, but they were mindful of his condition restricting him from excessive sexual activity. When they weren't having intercourse, Chad pleasured her in other ways.

He was so happy because his knack for making a woman excited seemed to be revived.

Everything was going well until that fateful morning when Marge went to his bedroom to wake him. She was concerned because it was nine and he wasn't still up. Normally, he was up by seven thirty. Marge saw that he appeared to be lifeless and shook him, to no avail. Chad had died in his sleep.

Senator Rutter was immediately notified and made it to Salem that same day. The children were notified and removed temporarily from the witness protection program so they could attend their father's funeral.

The services were private and somewhat brief but this time much too real. Bishop Braden had outlived his brother and now was showing signs of senility. He was able to get through a very short version of a Catholic burial ceremony. After a get-together and a memorial Mass at the cathedral, both families returned to their respective locations. They were hoping to be reunited now that their dad was gone, and Mike Rutter vowed to work on it.

About two months later Senator Mike brought them together at a secured area of the Oklahoma Fairgrounds. The purpose was to discuss a plan to get them back to a normal existence.

Both families arrived, and when Sherry Ann saw her aunt Edie, she ran to her and yelled, "Aunt Edie, I miss you so much!"

From that moment on, the decision was inevitable: they must free themselves and live like a family once again. But how?

That was when Mark set a plan into motion. He said, "Dad left us some serious money, and I'll take a one-year sabbatical to work toward my PhD in criminal law. I'll study Dad's records and investigations so we can finally identify the enemy. As of now it could be the Russians or anyone else. Remember how Dad used to tell us how he destroyed the Russian mob? So maybe it's another group. I have asked Senator Mike to have me assigned to the Oklahoma FBI office so I can work with them."

Edie answered, "But you have no training in that field. Maybe you'll be risking your life."

Mark told her he was a fast learner and saw no drawback. His brother-in-law asked to join him but was turned down, especially now that Edie was pregnant. They all agreed to the plan and vowed to spend the next two days together having a lot of fun before returning to their safe havens. Senator Mike chimed in and exclaimed that he liked the plan. He made a point that he wanted his grandchild in his life and would make the necessary arrangements. Mark then requested that the FBI not be made aware of who he really was but only that he was a local guy writing a thesis for the government.

CHAPTER 34

After studying the players in his father's life, Mark was ready to go on the road. He now adopted the name of Mac Sully and started a jazz quintet. The group would be booked into areas where the suspects were. The hope was that the person or group so adverse to their father would be identified and summarily dealt with. He had now absorbed all the necessary information and felt prepared to embark on a perilous journey.

The first to be seen was Commander Richards from the old Buenos Aires days. He was living in Madison, Wisconsin, in a private nursing home run by the Sisters of Charity. Mark visited the facility and spoke to the Mother Superior. He was able to convince her that he was a long-lost nephew and wanted to see his uncle. She said his uncle had a severe case of dementia, but he could see for himself.

Upon entering the room, he saw someone who was now in a vegetative state awaiting that final moment. The trip was a loss as it was impossible to gain any information from him.

The next trip was to London where he met with the late Derek Hanson's wife. She remarried a minister and lived in a rather quaint village twenty miles south of the city. He introduced himself as a journalist who was writing a story about Chad Braden for the navy. After spending the better part of a day with Rita Hanson Jenkins, he knew this was another dead end. In fact, he was surprised how very little she wanted to share of that untimely death.

He then made a trip to South America to find and talk to Uncle John and his family. It was immediately made known to him that the farm had been sold and now the family was living in a luxurious apartment in the city. Upon visiting the complex, he again passed himself off as a journalist writing a story about Chad Braden. The father and mother had died, but Netta and Rosa were glad to talk to him but really had no relevant information. He was now in a negative three for three and went home hoping to get something solid soon.

A most difficult task was to locate Admiral Chancy's two gay sons. After they were exposed, they resigned from the service and were now living in Hawaii. Both had partners, and all had joint ownership of a Japanese lavish restaurant and night club. Mark was able to book his group into the night club through an international agency for four days. While there he was able to look them in the eyes and have several conversations with them. They were now very successful and having a great time living it up with their soul mates. Their present lifestyles did not reek of revenge, so Mark went on to someone else.

Having researched his father's murder trial, he decided to investigate Judge Mary Bryant and her children. He was also looking into Johnny Blaine's relatives. This investigation was centered in Maryland but he decided to do it from afar in fear of being recognized. So he fully utilized the FBI files and was able to make informed judgments. Judge Bryant had been released from jail and was living in Phoenix with her daughter. Mark went to Arizona for a personal stakeout and spent a few days trying to get a handle on that situation. The daughter was married to a man who owned a clothing store in town. When he saw Judge Bryant, he knew she was not a likely candidate. She was so frail. Mark wrote them off and had no further interest in that family. Johnny Blaine had died and his wife had remarried. They had no children. Another closed door.

That left two others to be investigated: Della Chancy and her niece, Mary Edison. This proved to be very difficult because they both had disappeared into the witness protection program years ago. He had to beg the librarian in the FBI building to retrieve the information. She was cute and well built. Mark took her to lunch twice and to bed once before she passed the information to him. The librarian turned out to be a hot number who enjoyed sex, especially the kinky perversions. She had made it known that only after their liaison would she give him what he wanted. It was a sacrifice on Mark's part, but he managed to survive it.

Della Chancy lived in Lake Tahoe, California, under the assumed name Bridget Harrison. She was a well-known novelist who wrote books but couldn't capitalize on her fame because she was in the witness protection program.

Mark booked his quartet at Harrah's, located on the Nevada side, for a weekend gig, hoping to visit her during his stay. Once arriving in the area, he found her address at a three-story lakefront house.

He decided to visit her and pose as an aficionado of her books and a student studying for a master's degree in American literature. He was able to get her telephone number and called her to set up a visit. When he got there, she was at the front door. He was taken in by her beauty and shape at her age of eighty.

Before he could say anything, she amazed him by blurting out, "You're not a student. I recognize that face—you're the spitting image of your father. My sons called me and warned you would be looking me up. They weren't fooled by your charade and played along with you. How is Chad these days? And what do you want from me?"

"My father passed away, and I'm trying to get peace for our family. Maybe you can help us?"

Della then said that she knew nothing and invited him in for a cup of tea. For the next hour, Mark listen as she told how Chad had messed up her whole life and career.

"Being in the witness protection program has estranged me from my boys, my sisters, and my nieces. Did I hate him? You bet I did. But that is all in the past. I give you my word that I no longer bear ill will toward your dad and his family. I'm an old woman and don't need that sort of thing in my life now."

Mark then asked about her niece, Mary Edison, but Della knew nothing of her. He left unimpressed with her attempt to convince him that she was separated from the past.

CHAPTER 35

CHAPTER 35

Mark returned to the librarian at the FBI office for the information on Mary Edison. She directed him to Agent Spence in the Lexington, Kentucky, office. When they met, Spence told him that Mary Edison was dead. He also said that Mary had married Jim Thompson, business manager of the Lexington Race Track. She had met him while working there as an accounting supervisor. When they were married some five years, Mary got word that her mom had died. Both decided to leave the witness protection program and motored to Maryland for the funeral.

The obituary named Mary and her twin sister, Margaret, as the only survivors. After the funeral, Jim and Mary went home via West Virginia and stopped at the Ramsey Motel. The maid found them murdered the next morning. The investigation showed that they were followed by a couple of thugs from a local restaurant. Mary was sporting a lot of expensive jewelry and Jim showing a wad of cash. The murderers were arrested within a couple of days holding the cash and jewelry.

"Do you have anything on her sister? What about the father?"

Spence answered that the father was dead and her sister, Margaret, was living in the Washington DC area and her married name was Felton.

Mark said thanks and at the same time felt a horrible pain in his gut. He said to himself, "She killed my father."

Mark had always had bad vibes about Marge, especially when he discovered she was sleeping with Chad. He then reasoned that it was easy for her to poison him or induce the heart attack that killed him. The fact that it was reported as a heart attack resulted in no autopsy being performed. It would be tough to prove her involvement, and the only move left was to exhume Chad's body. He called Senator Rutter and asked to meet him in two days at the naval intelligence office in Washington DC.

The meeting came fast enough, and Mark easily convinced the others that Nurse Felton, a.k.a. Margaret Edison, could be the person responsible for the constant turmoil in their lives. All agreed that it was just too much of a coincidence that she appeared as Chad's nurse.

He then presented a plan that could be implemented rather quickly. Mark suggested he visit Marge in her Boston apartment under the guise of capturing for the family an account of his father's last days. He would wear a wire, and the FBI would be camping outside nearby in an unmarked van. In the event they were needed, their response would be immediate.

Marge would be told that the body had been exhumed and that there was conclusive proof that she murdered Chad. He would suggest that the authorities would be willing to offer a life sentence instead of death. Obviously it was a bluff, but maybe there was a chance that she would take the bait. The FBI thought Mark was taking too many chances and offered to have an agent accompany him to the meeting. He refused because she would not open up to a stranger. He then called and made an appointment to see her.

Mark had a further thought relative to the recorder. He would have two, one on the table and the other on his person. He would then unplug the one on the table for Marge's benefit.

He took the Amtrak train to Boston and arrived at noon after a very comfortable journey. The cab ride was uneventful, and he arrived at 1:00 p.m. as promised. She rang back the buzzer and opened the door for him.

Marge offered Mark a drink. "A Coke would be fine."

She went into the kitchen and brought back a tall glass of Coke. Mark was rather thirsty, took a large sip, put the glass down, and said, "Let me be blunt. We think you killed my father. His body has been exhumed, and the recovered evidence is enough to earn you a trip to death row. If you tell me all, I've been authorized by the government to offer you a life sentence. Here is the document granting that authority."

She took it, read it, and without batting an eyelash began to speak. "Before I tell you anything, turn off the recorder on the table." When he did, she continued. "My aunt Della orchestrated this plot against your dad and his family. We lost my uncle; my sister, Mary, and her husband, and my mother was never the same. My father went to his grave with his mind gone because of pain and sadness. Not to mention the humiliation my gay cousins suffered when they were outed and forced to resign from the navy. They were responsible for hiring that Iranian fellow who botched the stabbing of Chad at the hospital. When that failed, they hired two others to bomb the bus you were on and kidnap your brother-in-law.

"Both attempts were screwed up, so my aunt told me that I was the only person who could get to your father. I agreed because of my burning hatred of Chad and promoted myself to be his nurse. I took a position at the hospital and when I heard that he was going to Salem, I went to see Jack Slater. I knew he was close to Senator Rutter and would be able to get me an appointment with him. Jack recommended me, and the Senator hired me on the spot. I became his therapy nurse. We were constantly together, and I noticed that he was looking at me sexually. So to gain his confidence, I slept with him.

"After that, I decided to complete my task. A nurse friend of mine had told me of a liquid called potassium chloride that, once ingested, would induce a heart attack. That last night of his life, I put it into his tea and kissed him good night, and he was dead by morning. Was I happy? Yes. Why am I telling you all of this? Because I have done the same thing to you. I spiked your Coke with two tablespoons of antifreeze. The drink was sweeter than usual, but you never caught on. Unfortunately, you will never make it back to your hotel. Maybe you were thinking I was afraid of dying and that's why I was spilling my guts. No way, Jose. Now Aunt Della will be very proud of me. I got two Bradens now."

Mark then started to feel faint and was on the verge of passing out. Fortunately, the FBI agents were listening and immediately summoned an ambulance. The hospital was informed that antifreeze had been used and they could produce an antidote. The agents advanced to Marge's apartment and broke down the door.

She was flabbergasted as she never realized someone was listening in on her confession, which included implicating her aunt and cousins. Marge offered no excuse, defense, or remorse for her behavior. Her only statement was a request for her lawyer.

CHAPTER 36

They rushed an unconscious Mark to Boston General. The doctors were waiting for him but had not yet formulated an antidote for the poison. In addition, his blood pressure was dangerously low. About an hour later, the doctors administered what was considered a viable antidote. However, it didn't really take, other than to cause a spike in his blood pressure. His condition was critical. In intensive care, his life signs were monitored on a moment-to-moment basis. While he lay in a coma, he was being fed the antidote.

His family was with him every day waiting for a sign of life and hoping he would come to. Each day presented a different array of problems, such as a catheter infection and bedsores.

Finally, when there seemed to be no hope left, Sherry Ann noticed that her dad's eyes had opened. She was very excited, calling her mom and the nurses on duty.

The first thing he uttered was, "What happened to me?"

The nurses and doctors were able to explain his condition to him and he appeared calmer. From that point onward it was medication and therapy to bring him back to a state of normalcy. It was a tough road, but after three weeks, he was ready to go home to Maryland.

June had moved the family from Oklahoma to Townsend where she had rented a great house with an option to buy. But she was not a happy camper, voicing her displeasure about the quality of their life.

"I can't take it anymore. We've never been safe, and I'm sick and tired of looking over my shoulders for the next tragedy."

Mark promised her that it was all over soon, to which she said, "If not, I'm leaving you."

Edie and John came back from their Texas relocation home and had their first child, a boy named Chad.

Bishop Braden went to a priest retirement home in Baltimore. It wasn't long after that he became a victim of senility and diabetes.

Marge Felton and Della Chancy pleaded guilty in exchange for life sentences.

The gay sons vanished from Hawaii and were believed to be living on a remote island in the Pacific.

Once Mark was back to health, he decided to follow up on an offer to settle in the New York studio recording industry. He would receive a lucrative salary and upscale housing in the high-end community of Pelham, New York. But June wanted no part of the move and was adamant about remaining in Maryland near to her aging parents.

They finally agreed that Mark would commute home every weekend until they could work it out. That never happened because June finally confessed that she was no longer in love with Mark. She had met a man who was a fellow teacher at the school in Oklahoma, and he recently moved to Maryland to be near June.

The divorce was amicable and final within months. It was not a pleasant time for Mark— he'd almost lost his life, marriage, and family. He tried to be positive about the situation but could not help but think a black cloud loomed over him, just as it did during his father's life. After many sessions with psychologists, Mark realized it was up to him to shake those feelings of despair. He now felt good about himself, crediting the change to the medication.

However, after several months he decided to abandon the medication. The end came too fast as he was on the train platform in Pelham on his way to see his daughter, Sherry Ann, when he was struck by a westbound train. He died from injuries at the scene. There were no witnesses; Mark had been alone on the platform. What happened will always remain a mystery.

The date was February 19, his father's and uncle's birthdates. Just like Chad, the nineteenth had haunted him forever.

Printed in the United States
By Bookmasters